'I don't want a wife. **I require a woman to marry me and have my child. We will then separate and divorce and my life will return to normal again.'**

'And what about the child?' Pixie asked with a frown of dismay towards Apollo. 'What will happen to the child in all this?'

'The child will remain with its mother and I will attempt to be an occasional father to the best of my ability. My goal is to negotiate a civilised and workable arrangement with the woman of my choice.'

'You do indeed have a problem,' she commented, with a certain amount of amusement at Apollo's predicament. 'But I really don't understand why you're confiding in *me* of all people!'

'Are you always this slow on the uptake?'

Her smooth brow indented as she sipped her wine and looked up at him enquiringly from below her spidery lashes. 'What do you mean?'

She had beautiful eyes, Apollo acknowledged in surprise, eyes of a luminous clear grey that shone like polished silver in certain lights.

'What do you think I'm doing here with you?' he prompted huskily.

Christmas with a Tycoon

Mediterranean billionaires under the mistletoe

Christmas might be a time for giving, but these
billionaires are thinking only of what they can take!

Vito Zaffari might have a ruthless reputation,
but when Holly crashes his festive hideaway she leaves
with an unexpected Christmas gift…

Apollo Metraxis has made a career of bachelorhood,
but the conditions of his father's will force him to
choose a bride. Pixie might be the last wife he'd
ever choose, but she's soon the only one he wants!

Don't miss either of these fabulous festive stories!

The Italian's Christmas Child
November 2016

The Greek's Christmas Bride
December 2016

Available now!

THE GREEK'S CHRISTMAS BRIDE

BY
LYNNE GRAHAM

MILLS
BOON

First Published in Great Britain 2016
By Mills & Boon, an imprint of HarperCollins*Publishers*
1 London Bridge Street, London, SE1 9GF

© 2016 Lynne Graham

ISBN: 978-0-263-06581-7

Our policy is to use papers that are natural, renewable and recyclable
products and made from wood grown in sustainable forests. The logging
and manufacturing processes conform to the legal environmental
regulations of the country of origin.

Printed and bound in Great Britain
by CPI Antony Rowe, Chippenham, Wiltshire

Lynne Graham was born in Northern Ireland and has been a keen romance reader since her teens. She is very happily married to an understanding husband who has learned to cook since she started to write! Her five children keep her on her toes. She has a very large dog who knocks everything over, a very small terrier who barks a lot, and two cats. When time allows, Lynne is a keen gardener.

Books by Lynne Graham

Mills & Boon Modern Romance

Bought for the Greek's Revenge
The Sicilian's Stolen Son
Leonetti's Housekeeper Bride
The Secret His Mistress Carried
The Dimitrakos Proposition
A Ring to Secure His Heir
Unlocking Her Innocence

Christmas with a Tycoon

The Italian's Christmas Child

The Notorious Greeks

The Greek Demands His Heir
The Greek Commands His Mistress

Bound by Gold

The Sheikh's Secret Babies
The Billionaire's Bridal Bargain

The Legacies of Powerful Men

Ravelli's Defiant Bride
Christakis's Rebellious Wife
Zarif's Convenient Queen

Visit the Author Profile page at millsandboon.co.uk for more titles.

I do enjoy an alpha male,
but none of them is a match for my husband.
This one is for you.

PROLOGUE

THE MALE VOICES drifted in from the balcony while Holly hovered, waiting uneasily for the right moment to join the conversation. That was a challenge when she knew she was never particularly welcome in Apollo's radius.

But there wasn't much she could do about that when she was married to Vito, Apollo's best friend. Only recently had she come to appreciate just how close the two men were and how often they talked no matter where they were in the world. Friends from a childhood spent at boarding school, they were as close as brothers and Apollo had distrusted Holly from the outset because she was a poor woman marrying a very rich man. Aware of that fact, she had offered to stay home instead of attending the funeral of Apollo's father but Vito had been shocked at that suggestion.

So far, their visit to the privately owned island of Nexos and the Metraxis compound had been anything but pleasant. The funeral had been massive. Every one of Apollo's former stepmothers and their children had attended. Earlier today the reading of the will had taken place and Apollo had stormed out in a passion, having learned that he needed a wife to inherit the vast empire he had been running for several years on his ailing father's behalf. Vito had shared only that bare detail with his wife, clearly uncomfortable at divulging even that much. But as virtually anybody who knew Apollo also knew of his aversion to matrimony, it was obvious that his father's last will and testament had put him between a rock and a hard place.

'So, you pick one of your women and marry her,' Vito breathed, sounding not at all like the loving husband Holly knew and adored. '*Dio mio*, there's a long enough list. You marry her, stay married as long as you can bear it, and—'

'And how am I going to get rid of her again?' Apollo growled. 'Women cling to me like superglue. How am I going to trust her to keep her mouth shut? If word escapes that it's a fake marriage, the stepfamilies will go to court and try and take my inheritance off me. If you tell a woman you don't want her, she's insulted and she wants revenge.'

'That's why you need to *hire* a wife as if you're interviewing one for a job. You need a woman with no personal axe to grind. Considering your popularity with the opposite sex and your bad reputation, finding her could be a challenge.'

Reckoning that it was now or never, Holly stepped out onto the terrace. 'Hiring a wife sounds like the best idea,' she opined nervously.

Even sheathed in an elegant dark suit, Apollo Metraxis looked every inch the bad boy he was. With shoulder-length black hair, startling green eyes and an elaborate dragon tattoo peeping out of a white shirt cuff, Apollo was volatile, unconventional and arrogant, the direct opposite of Holly's conservative husband.

'I don't believe you were invited to join this conversation,' Apollo countered very drily.

'Three heads are better than two,' Holly parried, forcing herself down stiffly into a seat.

Apollo elevated a sardonic brow. 'You think so?'

Holly refused to be excluded. 'Stop dramatising yourself—'

'Holly!' Vito interrupted sharply.

'Well, Apollo can't help himself. He's always doing it,' Holly argued. 'Not every woman is going to cling to you like superglue!'

'Name me one who won't,' Apollo invited.

Holly blinked and thought very hard because Apollo was universally acknowledged to be a gorgeous, super-wealthy stud and nine out of ten women followed him round a room with hungry eyes. 'Well, my friend Pixie for a start,' she pronounced with satisfaction. 'She can't stand you and if she can't, there's got to be others.'

A very faint flush accentuated Apollo's supermodel cheekbones.

'Pixie wouldn't quite meet the parameters of what is required,' Vito interposed hastily, meeting his friend's appalled gaze in a look of mutual understanding because he had not told his wife the exact terms of the will. Ignorant as Holly was of those terms, she could not know how impossible her suggestion was.

Apollo was outraged by the reference to Holly's friend, Pixie, who was a hairdresser and poor as a peasant. Apollo already knew everything there was to know about Holly and Pixie because he had had the two women thoroughly investigated as soon as Holly appeared out of nowhere to announce that she had given birth to Vito's son, Angelo. Apollo had been appalled by Pixie's grubby criminal background and the debts her unsavoury brother had accrued and which she for some strange reason had chosen to take on as her own. Those debts had resulted in her brother's punishment beating and her attempt to interfere with that had put Pixie in a wheelchair with two broken legs.

Was it any wonder that when her friend had such a bad background he had instinctively distrusted Holly and marvelled at his friend's eagerness to marry the mother of his child? Indeed Apollo had been waiting on the sidelines ever since for Pixie to try and take advantage of her friendship with Holly by approaching her friend for financial help. To date, however, she had not done so and Apollo had been relieved for he had no desire to interfere again, knowing how much that would be resented. And thanks to his ungenerous attitude at their wedding, Holly already resented Apollo quite enough.

Pixie Robinson, Apollo thought again in wonderment as Vito and Holly retreated indoors to change for dinner. He was unlikely to forget the tiny doll-like blonde in the wheelchair at Vito's wedding. She had given Apollo nothing but dirty looks throughout the day and had really irritated him. Holly was insane. Of course she was biased, Pixie being her best friend and all that, but even so, could she really imagine Apollo marrying Pixie and them producing an heir together? Apollo almost shuddered before he reminded himself that Holly didn't know about that most outrageous demand in his father's will.

He had seriously underestimated the older man, Apollo conceded angrily. Vassilis Metraxis had always had a bee in his bonnet about the continuation of the family name, hence his six marriages and unsuccessful attempts to have another child. At thirty, Apollo was an only child. His father had urged his son to marry many times and Apollo had been blunt and honest about his resolve to remain single and childless. In spite of the depredations of the manipulative, grasping stepmothers and the greedy stepchildren that had come with those marriages, Apollo had always enjoyed a relatively close and loving relationship with his father. For that reason, the terms of Vassilis's will had come as a very nasty shock.

According to the will, Apollo was to continue running his father's empire and enjoying his possessions but that state of affairs was guaranteed to continue only for the next five years. Within that period Apollo had to legally marry and produce a child if he wanted to retain his inheritance. If he failed on either count, the Metraxis wealth would be shared out amongst his father's ex-wives and former stepchildren even though they had all been richly rewarded while his father was still alive.

Apollo could not credit that his father had been so foolish as to try and blackmail his son from beyond the grave. And yet wasn't it proving most effective? Rigid with tension as he made that sudden leap in understanding, Apollo stood on the terrace looking out to sea and watching the stormy waves batter the cliffs. His grandfather had bought the island of Nexos and built the villa for family use. Every Metraxis since then had been buried in the little graveyard down by the village church, including Apollo's mother, who had died in childbirth.

The island was Apollo's home, the only real home he had ever known, and he was disconcerted to realise that he literally could not *bear* the idea of his home being sold off, which would mean that he could never visit it or his memories again. He was discovering way too late to change anything that he was far more attached to the family name and the family property than he had ever dreamt. He had fought the prospect of marriage, habitually mocking the institution and rubbishing his father's unsuccessful attempts to recreate a normal family circle. He had sworn that he would never father a child, for as a child Apollo had suffered a great deal and he had genuinely believed that it would be wrong to subject any child to what he had endured. Yet from beyond the grave his father had contrived to call his bluff...

For when it came down to it, Apollo could not contemplate losing the world he took for granted even though he knew that fighting to retain it would be a hellish struggle. A struggle against his own volatile inclinations and his innate love of freedom, a struggle against being *forced* to live with a woman, *forced* to have sex with her, *forced* to have a child he didn't want.

And how best could he achieve that? Unfortunately, Vito was right: Apollo needed to hire a woman, one who was willing to marry him solely for money. But how could he trust such a woman not to go to the media to spill all or to confide his secrets in the wrong person? He would need a *hold* on the woman he married, some sort of a hold that meant she needed him as much as he needed her and would have good reason to follow any rules he laid down.

Although he would never consider her as a possibility, he *needed* a woman like Pixie Robinson. In her case he could have bought up her brother's debt and used it to put pressure on her, thereby ensuring that it was in her best interests to keep her mouth shut and give him exactly what he needed to retain his family empire. How was he supposed to find another woman in that kind of situation?

Of course, had he trusted women generally, he might have been less cautious. But Apollo, his cynical distrust honed over no fewer than six stepmothers and countless lovers, had never trusted a woman in his life. In fact trust was a real issue for him.

His first stepmother had sent him off to boarding school at the age of four. His second stepmother had beaten him bloody. His third had seduced him. His fourth

stepmother had had his beloved dog put down. His fifth
stepmother had tried to foist another man's child on his
father.

Add in the innumerable women whom Apollo had
bedded over the years. Beautiful, sexually adventurous
women and gold-diggers, who had endeavoured to enrich
themselves as much as possible during their brief affairs
with him. He had never known any other kind of woman,
couldn't quite believe that any other type existed. Holly
was different though, he acknowledged grudgingly. He
could see that she adored Vito and their child. So, there
was another category out there: women who *loved*. Not
that he would be looking for one of those. Love would
trap him, inhibit him and suffocate him with the dos and
don'ts he despised. He suppressed a shudder. Life was
too short to make such a mistake.

But in the short term he still needed a wife. A wife he
could *control* was the only sort of wife he would be able
to tolerate. He thought about Pixie again. Pixie and her
weak, feckless brother's financial problems. She had to
be pretty stupid, he reflected helplessly, to mess up her
life by taking on her sibling's problems. Why would you
do that? Never having had a brother or a sister, Apollo
was mystified by the concept of such thankless sacrifice. But just how far would Pixie Robinson go to save
her brother's skin?

It amused Apollo to know so much more than Holly
did about her best friend's problems. It amused him even
more that Holly had cheerfully assured him that Pixie
couldn't stand him. Holly had to be blind. Obviously
Holly hadn't noticed that, in spite of the dirty looks, Pixie
had covertly watched Apollo's every move at her friend's
wedding.

The beginnings of a smile softened the hard line of

Apollo's wide sensual mouth. Maybe he should take a closer look at the miniature blonde and work out whether or not she could be of use to him…what did he have to lose?

CHAPTER ONE

'MORNING, HECTOR,' PIXIE mumbled as she woke up with a tousled bundle of terrier plastered to her ribs.

Smothering a yawn, she steeled herself to get up and out. She got out of bed to head to the bathroom she shared with the other tenants on the same floor before returning washed and dressed to snap a leash on Hector's faded red collar and take her pet out for his morning walk.

Hector trotted along the road, little round eyes reflecting anxiety. He flinched when he noticed another dog across the street. Hector was scared of just about everything life threw at him. People, other animals, traffic and loud noises all made the whites of his eyes gleam with an edge of panic. Calm and untroubled the rest of the time, he was very quiet and had never been known to bark.

'Probably learned not to as a puppy,' the vet next door to the hair salon had opined when Pixie had asked. 'He's scared of attracting attention to himself in any way. Abuse does that to an animal. But in spite of his injuries he's young and healthy and should have a long life ahead of him.'

Pixie still marvelled at the fact that regardless of her own problems she had chosen to adopt Hector. But then, Pixie had triumphed over adversity many times in life and so had the little terrier. Hector had repaid her generosity a thousand times over. He comforted her and warmed her heart with his shy little ways and eccentricities. He had filled some of the giant hole that had opened up in Pixie's world when Holly and Angelo had moved to Italy.

She had lost her best friend to marriage and motherhood but their friendship had been more damaged by the secrets Pixie had been forced to keep. There was no way she could tell Holly about her brother Patrick's gambling debts without Holly offering to settle those debts for them. Holly was very generous but Patrick was not Holly or Vito's responsibility, he was Pixie's and had been since the day of their mother's death.

'Promise me you'll look after your little brother,' Margery Robinson had pleaded. 'Always do your best for Patrick, Pixie. He's a gentle soul and he's the only family you have left.'

But looking after Patrick had been near impossible when the siblings had invariably ended up living in different foster homes. During the important teenaged years, Pixie had only met up with her brother a handful of times and until she'd finished training and achieved independence her bond with her kid brother had been limited by time, distance and a shortage of money. Once she was working she had tried to change all that by regularly visiting Patrick in London.

Initially Patrick had done well. He was an electrician working for a big construction firm. He had found a girlfriend and settled down. But he had also got involved in high-stake card games and had lost a lot of money to a very dangerous man. Pixie had duly cut down her own expenses, moving out of the comfortable terraced house she had once shared with Holly into a much cheaper bedsit. Every week she sent as much money as she could afford to Patrick to help him pay off his debts but as interest was added that debt just seemed to be getting bigger and if he missed a payment he would be beaten up... or worse. Pixie genuinely feared that her brother's debts would get him killed.

Pixie still came out in a cold sweat remembering the night the debt collectors had arrived when she had been visiting her brother. Two big brutish men had come to the door of Patrick's flat to demand money. Threatening to kill him, they had beaten him up when he was unable to pay his dues. Attempting to intervene in the ensuing struggle, Pixie had fallen down the stairs and broken both her legs. The consequences of that accident had been horrendous because Pixie had been unable to work and had been forced to claim benefits during her recovery. Now, six months on, she was just beginning to get back to normal but unhappily there seemed to be no light gleaming at the end of the tunnel because Patrick's debt situation seemed insurmountable and his life was still definitely at risk. The man he owed wasn't the type to wait indefinitely for settlement. He would want his pound of flesh or he would want to make an example of her brother to intimidate his other debtors.

Settling Hector into his basket, Pixie set off down the street to the hair salon. She missed her car but selling Clementine had been her first sacrifice because she had no real need for personal transport in the small Devon town where she could walk most places. She would return home to take Hector out for a walk during her lunch break and grab a sandwich at the same time.

Entering the salon, she exchanged greetings with her co-workers and her boss, Sally. After hurriedly stowing her bag in her staff locker she caught a glimpse of herself in a mirror and winced. It had been a while since she had looked her best. When had she got so boring? She was only twenty-three years old. Unfortunately cutting costs had entailed wearing her clothes for longer and her jeans and black top had seen better days. She had good skin and didn't wear much make-up but she always wore loads of grey eyeliner because black liner was too stark against the blonde hair that fell simply to just below her shoulders. She had left behind her more adventurous days of playing with different styles and colours because she had soon come to appreciate that most of her clients had conservative tastes and were nervous of a hairdresser who had done anything eye-catching to her own hair.

She cleaned up after her third client had departed. She regretted the reality that yet another junior had walked out, leaving the stylists to deal with answering the phone, washing hair and sweeping up. She checked the appointment book for her next booking and, unusually, she didn't recognise the name. It was a guy though and she was surprised he hadn't asked for the only male stylist in the salon. And then, without the smallest warning, Apollo Metraxis walked in and as every female jaw literally dropped in wonderment and silence spread like the plague he strode up to Pixie and announced, 'I'm your twelve o'clock appointment.'

Pixie gaped at him, not quite sure it could actually be him in the flesh. 'What the heck are you doing here? Has something happened to Holly or Vito?' she demanded apprehensively.

'I need a trim,' Apollo announced levelly, perfectly comfortable with the fact that he was the cynosure of every eye in the place. Clad in a black biker jacket, tight jeans and boots, he seemed impossibly tall as he towered over her, bright green eyes strikingly noticeable in his lean bronzed face.

'Holly? Vito? Angelo?' Pixie pressed with staccato effect, her attention glued to his broad chest and the tee shirt plastered to his six-pack abs.

'As far as I know they're all well,' Apollo retorted impatiently.

But that still didn't explain what a Greek billionaire was doing walking into a high-street hair salon in a small country town where as far as she was aware he knew nobody. And she couldn't be counted because he had never spoken to her, never even so much as glanced at her on the day of Holly's wedding. The memory rankled because she was only human, whether she liked it or not. After trying to ruin Holly's wedding for her by making an embarrassing speech in his role of best man, he had royally ignored Pixie as if she was beneath his lofty notice.

'I'm afraid I have another appointment.'

'That's me. *John Smith?* Didn't you smell a rat?' he mocked.

In actuality the only thing Pixie could smell that close to Apollo was Apollo and the alluring scent of some no doubt very expensive citrusy designer cologne.

'Let me take your jacket,' she said jerkily, struggling to regain her composure and behave normally.

He shrugged it off, more powerful muscles bunching and flexing with his every movement. He exposed the bare arm with the intricate dragon tattoo that had made her stare at her friend's wedding. Then she hurriedly turned away and hung the heavy leather jacket on the coat stand beside the reception desk.

'Come over to the sinks,' Pixie urged, alarmingly short of breath at the prospect of laying actual hands on him.

Apollo stared down at her. She was even smaller than he had expected, barely reaching his chest and very delicate in build. He had seen boards with more curves. But

she had amazing eyes, a light grey that glittered like stolen starlight in her expressive face. She had an undistin-
guished button nose and a full rosebud mouth while her
flawless skin had the translucent glow of the finest porcelain. She was much more natural than the women he was
accustomed to. Definitely no breast enhancements, no
fake tan and even her mouth appeared to be all her own.

As he sat down Pixie whisked a cape round him and
then a towel, determined not to be intimidated by him.
'So, what on earth are you doing here?'

'You'll never guess,' Apollo intoned, tilting his head
back for her.

Pixie ran the water while noting that he had the most
magnificent head of hair. Layers and layers of luxuriant
blue-black glossy strands. His mocking response tightened her mouth and frustration gripped her. 'When did
you last see our mutual friends?' she asked instead.

'At my father's funeral last week,' Apollo advanced.

Pixie stiffened. 'I'm sorry for your loss,' she said immediately.

'Why should you be sorry?' Apollo asked with un-
settling derision. 'You didn't know him and you don't
know me.'

Her teeth gritted at that scornful dismissal as she
shampooed his hair. 'It's just what people say to show
sympathy.'

'*Are* you sympathetic?'

Pixie was tempted to drench him with the shower head
she was using. Her teeth ground together even tighter.
'I'm sympathetic to anyone who's lost a family member.'

'He was dying for a long time,' Apollo admitted flatly.
'It wasn't unexpected.'

His outrageously long fringe of black lashes flicked
down over his striking eyes and she got on with her job

on automatic pilot while her mind seethed with questions. What did he want with her? Was it foolish of her to think that his descent on the place where she worked had to relate to her personally? Yet how could it relate to her? Outside her ties to Holly and Vito, there was no possible connection.

'Tell me about you,' Apollo invited, disconcerting her.

'Why would I?'

'Because I asked…because it's polite?' he prompted, his posh British upper-class accent smooth as glass.

'Let's talk about you instead,' she suggested. 'What are you doing in England?'

'A little business, a little socialising. Visiting friends,' he responded carelessly.

She applied conditioner and embarked on a head massage with tautly nervous fingers. A second after she began she realised she had not asked him if he wanted one but she kept going all the same, desperate to take charge of the encounter and keep busy.

Apollo relaxed while lazily wondering if she did any other kind of massage. The file hadn't shed much light on her sex life or her habits but then two broken legs had kept her close to home for months. As her slender fingers moved rhythmically across his skull he pictured her administering to him buck naked and the sudden tightening at his groin warned him to give it a rest.

Irritated by the effect she was having on his highly tense body, Apollo thought about how much he needed sex to wind down. His last liaison had ended before his father's funeral and he had not been with anyone since then. Unlike Vito, Apollo never went without sex. A couple of weeks was a very long time for him. Had he found Pixie unattractive, he would've backed off straight away; however that wasn't the case. But—*Diavole!*—she was teeny, tiny as a doll and he was a big guy in every way. She rinsed his hair and towelled him dry while he thought about her hands on his body and that ripe bee-stung mouth taking him to climax. It was a relief to move and settle down in another chair.

'What do you want done?' she asked him after she had combed his hair.

He almost told her because he was all revved up and ready to go and he had never before reacted to a woman with such unsophisticated schoolboyish enthusiasm. 'A trim...but leave it long,' he warned her while he wondered what the secret of her attraction was.

Novelty value? He was tall and he generally went for tall, curvy blondes. But possibly he had got bored with a steady diet of women so similar they had become almost interchangeable. Vito had raved about how down-to-earth and unspoilt Holly was but Apollo was a great deal less high flown in his expectations. If Pixie pleased him in bed, he would count her a prize. If she got pregnant quickly he would treat her like a princess. If she gave him a child, she would live like a lottery winner. Apollo believed in only rewarding results.

Of course, she might turn him down. A woman had never turned him down before but he knew there had to be a first time and it was not as though he were in the habit of asking women to have a child with him. And if he spilled all to Pixie then he would be vulnerable because she might choose to share his secrets with the media for a handsome price and that would scupper his plans. So, however she reacted, he would be stuck having to pay her to keep quiet and that reality and the risk involved annoyed him.

Momentarily, Pixie stepped away to right the swaying coat stand, knocked off balance by an elderly woman. In the mirror, Apollo watched as Pixie bent down to pick up and hang the coats that had fallen and he was riveted by a glimpse of her curvy little rump before she straightened and returned to his side.

Her scissors went snip-snip. She was confident with what she did and every so often her fingers would smooth through his hair in a gesture almost like a caress. He glanced at her from below his lashes, wondering if it was a come-on, but her heart-shaped face was intent on her task, her eyes veiled, her mouth a tense line. It didn't stop Apollo imagining those touchy-feely hands roaming freely over him. In fact the more he thought about that, the hotter he got.

When she wielded the drier over him, Apollo tried to take it off her. He usually dried his own hair and then damped it down again to make it presentable but Pixie swore she would do nothing fancy and withheld the drier, determined to personally tame his messy mane.

Until she had had the experience of cutting Apollo's hair it had never crossed Pixie's mind that her job could be an unsettlingly intimate one. But touching Apollo's surprisingly silky hair disturbed her, making her aware of him on a level she was very uncomfortable with. He smelled so damned good she wanted to sniff him in like an intoxicating draught of sunshine. Wide shoulders flexed as he settled back in the chair and she sucked in a slow steadying breath. She had never been so on edge with a customer in her life. Her nipples were tight inside her bra and she felt embarrassingly damp between her thighs.

No, she absolutely was *not* attracted to Apollo. It was simply that he made her very nervous. The guy was a literal celebrity, an international playboy adored by the media for his jet-set womanising lifestyle. Any normal woman would feel overwhelmed by his sudden appearance. It was like having a lion walk into the room, she reflected wildly. You couldn't stop staring, you couldn't do less than admire his animal beauty and magnificence but not far underneath lurked a ferocious fear of what he might do next.

Apollo sprang upright and Pixie hastened to retrieve his jacket and hand it to him. He stilled at the reception desk and dug inside it while she waited for him to pay. He frowned, black brows pleating, and stared at her. 'My wallet's gone,' he told her.

'Oh, dear...' Pixie muttered blankly.

His green eyes narrowed to shards of emerald cutting glass ready to draw blood. 'Did you take it?'

'Did I take your wallet?' In the wake of that echo of an answer, Pixie's mouth dropped open in shock because her brain was telling her that he could not possibly have accused her of stealing from him.

'You're the only person who touched my jacket,' Apollo condemned loud enough to turn heads nearby. 'Give it back and I'll take no action.'

'You've got to be out of your mind to think that I would *steal* from you!' Pixie exclaimed, stricken, as her boss, Sally, came rushing across the salon.

'I want the police called,' he informed the older woman grimly.

The dizziness of shock engulfed Pixie and she turned pale as death. She couldn't credit that Apollo was accusing her of theft in public. In fact her first thought was insane because she found herself wondering if he had come to the salon deliberately to set her up for such an accusation. All he had to do would be to leave his wallet behind and then accuse her of stealing from him. And who would believe her word against the word of someone of his wealth and importance?

Her stomach heaved and with a muffled groan she fled to the cloakroom to lose her breakfast. Apollo was subjecting her to her worst possible nightmare. Pixie had always had a pronounced horror of theft and dishonesty. Her father had been a serial burglar, in and out of prison all his life. Her mother had been a professional shoplifter, who stole to order. If Pixie had stumbled across a purse lying on the ground she would have walked past it, too terrified to pick it up and hand it in in case someone accused her of trying to steal it. It was a hangover from her shame-filled childhood and she had never yet contrived to overcome her greatest fear.

CHAPTER TWO

THE POLICEMAN WHO arrived was familiar—a middle-aged man who patrolled the streets of the small town. Pixie had seen him around but had never spoken to him because she gave the police a wide berth. Acquainted with most of the local traders, however, he was on comfortable terms with her boss, Sally.

By the time Apollo had been asked to give his name and details he was beginning to wonder if it had been a mistake to call in officialdom. He didn't want to be identified. He didn't want to risk the media getting involved. And if she *had* taken his wallet wasn't it really only the sort of behaviour he had expected from Pixie Robinson? She was desperate for money and he was well aware of the fact that his wallet would offer a bigger haul than most. The constable viewed him in astonishment when he admitted how much cash he had been carrying.

Pixie gave her name and address in a voice that trembled in spite of her attempt to keep it level. Sick with nerves, she shifted from one foot onto the other and then back again, unable to stay still, unable to meet anyone's eyes lest they recognise the panic consuming her. Perspiration beaded her short upper lip as the police officer asked her what had happened from the moment of Apollo's arrival. While she spoke she couldn't help noticing Apollo lounging back in an attitude of extravagant relaxation against the edge of the desk and occasionally glancing at his gold watch as though he had somewhere more important to be.

She had never been violent but Apollo filled her with vicious and aggressive reactions. How could he be so hateful and Vito still be friends with him? She had known Apollo wasn't a nice person on the day of Holly's wedding when his speech had made it obvious that Holly and Vito's son had been conceived from a one-night stand. Since then she had read more about him online. He was a womaniser who essentially didn't like women. She had recognised that reality straight off. His affairs never lasted longer than a couple of weeks. He got bored very quickly, never committed, indeed never got involved beyond the most superficial level.

'Don't forget to mention that you went back to the coat stand when the old lady knocked some of the coats to the floor,' Apollo reminded her in a languorous drawl.

'And you're suggesting that that's when I took your wallet?' Pixie snapped, studying him with eyes bright silver with loathing.

'Could it have fallen out of the jacket?' the police officer asked hopefully, tugging a couple of chairs out from the wall to glance behind them. 'Have you looked under the desk?'

'Not very likely,' Apollo traded levelly. 'Is no one going to search this woman? Her bag even?'

'Let's not jump to conclusions, Mr Metraxis,' the policeman countered quellingly as he lifted the rubbish bin.

Apollo raised an unimpressed brow. He was so judgemental and so confident that he was right, Pixie thought in consternation. He was absolutely convinced that she had stolen his wallet and it would take an earthquake to shift him. Her stomach lurched again and she crossed her arms defensively, the sick dizziness of fear assailing her once more. She didn't have his wallet but mud would stick. By tea time everyone local would know that the blonde stylist at Sally's had been accused of theft. At the very least she could lose her job. She wasn't so senior or talented that Sally would risk losing clients to her nearest competitor.

The policeman lifted the newspaper lying in the bin and, with an exclamation, he reached beneath it and lifted out a brown hide wallet. 'Is this it?'

Visibly surprised, Apollo extended his hand. 'Yes...'

'When the coat stand tipped, your wallet must've fallen out into the bin,' Sally suggested with a bright smile of relief at that sensible explanation.

'Or Pixie *hid* it in the bin to retrieve at a more convenient time,' Apollo murmured.

'This situation need not have arisen had a proper search been conducted before I was called in,' the policeman remarked. 'You were very quick to make an accusation, Mr Metraxis.'

Impervious to the hint of censure, Apollo angled his arrogant dark head back. 'I'm still not convinced my wallet ended up in the bin by accident,' he admitted. 'Pixie has a criminal background.'

Pixie froze in shocked mortification. How did Apollo Metraxis know that about her? That was private, that was her past and she had left it behind her a long time ago. 'But *not* a criminal record!' she flung back curtly, watching Apollo settle a bank note down on the desk and Sally hastily passing him his change.

'We shouldn't be discussing such things in public,' the policeman said drily and took his leave.

'Take the rest of the day off, Pixie,' Sally urged uncomfortably. 'I'm sorry I was so quick to call the police… but—'

'It's OK,' Pixie said chokily, well aware that her employer's business mantra was that the customer was always right and such an accusation had required immediate serious attention.

It was over. A faint shudder racked Pixie's slender frame. The nightmare was truly *over*. Apollo had his wallet back even though he still couldn't quite bring himself to accept that she hadn't stolen it and hidden it in the rubbish bin. But it *was* over and the policeman had departed satisfied. The fierce tension that had held Pixie still left her in a sudden rush and she could feel herself crumpling like rice paper inside and out as a belated surge of tears washed the backs of her eyelids.

'Excuse me,' she mumbled and fled to the back room to pull herself together and collect her bag.

She sniffed and wiped her eyes, knowing she was messing up her eyeliner and not even caring. She wanted to go home and hug Hector. Pulling on her jacket, she walked back through the salon, trying not to be self-conscious about the fact that the customers who had witnessed the little drama were all staring at her. A couple who knew her called out encouraging things but Pixie's entire attention was welded to the very tall male she could see waiting outside on the pavement. Why was Apollo still hanging around?

Of course, he wanted to apologise, she assumed. Why else would he be waiting? She stalked out of the door.

'Pixie?'

'You bastard!' she hissed at him in a raw undertone. 'Leave me alone!'

'I came here to speak to you—'

'Well, you've spoken to me and now you can...' Pixie swore at him, colliding with his scorching green eyes and almost reeling back from the anger she saw there.

'Get in the car. I'll take you home,' he said curtly.

Pixie swore at him again and, with a spluttering Greek curse and before she could even guess his intention, Apollo stooped and snatched her off her feet to carry her across the street.

Pixie thumped him so hard with her clenched fist, she hurt her knuckles.

'You're a violent little thing, aren't you?' Apollo framed rawly as he stuffed her in the back seat of the waiting limo.

'Let me out of this car!' Pixie gasped, flinging herself at the door on the opposite side as he slid in beside her.

'I'm taking you home,' Apollo countered, rubbing his cheekbone where it was turning slightly pink from her punch.

'I hope you get a black eye!' Pixie spat. 'Stop the car... let me out! This is kidnapping!'

'Do you really want to walk down the street with your make-up smeared all over your face?'

'Yes, if the alternative is getting a lift from you!'

But the limousine was already turning a corner to draw up outside the shabby building where she lived, so the argument was academic. As the doors unlocked, Pixie leapt out onto the pavement.

She might be petite in appearance but she was wiry and strong, Apollo acknowledged, and, not only did she know how to land a good punch, she also moved like greased lightning. He climbed out of the car at a more relaxed pace.

Breathing rapidly, Pixie paused in the hall with the door she had unlocked ajar. 'How did you know that about my background?'

'I'll tell you if you invite me in.'

'Why would I invite you in? I don't like you.'

'You know I can only be here to see you and you have to be curious,' Apollo responded with confidence.

'I can live with being curious,' Pixie told him, stepping into her room and starting to snap the door shut.

'But evidently you don't think you can live without your foolish little brother…do you?' Apollo drawled and the door stopped an inch off closing and slowing opened up again.

'What do you know about Patrick?' Pixie asked angrily.

Apollo strode in. 'I know everything there is to know about you, your brother, your background and your friend Holly. I had you both privately investigated when Holly first appeared out of nowhere with baby Angelo.'

Pixie studied him in shock and backed away several feet, which took her to the side of her bed. Even with the bed pushed up against one wall it was a small room. She had sold off much of the surplus stuff she had gathered up over the years before moving in. 'Why would you have us both investigated?' she exclaimed.

'I'm more cautious than Vito. I wanted to know who he was dealing with so that if necessary I could advise and protect him,' Apollo retorted with a slight shrug of a broad shoulder as he peered into a dark corner where something pale with glimmering eyes was trying to shrink into the wall.

'Just ignore Hector. Visitors, particularly male ones, freak him out,' Pixie told him thinly. 'I should think that Vito is old enough to protect himself.'

'Vito doesn't know much about the dark side of life.'

It was no surprise that Apollo considered himself superior in that regard, Pixie conceded. From childhood, scandal had illuminated Apollo's life to the outside world: his family's wealth, his father's many marriages to beautiful women half his age, the break-ups, the divorces and the court battles that had followed. Apollo's whole life had been lived in a histrionic headline-grabbing storm of publicity.

And there he stood in her little room, the perfect figurehead for a Greek billionaire, a living legend of a playboy with a yacht known to attract an exceptional number of gorgeous half-naked women. It seemed unfair that a male with such wealth and possessed of such undoubted intelligence should also have been blessed with such intense good looks. Apollo, like his namesake the sun god, was breathtakingly handsome. And he had undeniably taken Pixie's breath away the first time she'd seen him at Holly's wedding.

Apollo might be a toxic personality but when he was around he would always be the centre of attention. He had sleek dark brows, glorious green eyes, a classic nose and a stubborn, wilful mouth that could only be described as sensual. His sex appeal was electrifying and it was a sex appeal that Pixie would very much have liked to be impervious to. Sadly, however, she was a normal living, breathing woman with the usual healthy dose of hormones. And that was all it was…the breathlessness, the crazy race of her heartbeat, the tight fullness of her breasts and that strange squirmy, sensitive feeling low in her pelvis. It was all hormonal and as reflexive and trivial in Apollo's radius as her liking for chocolate, not something she needed to beat herself up about.

A faint little pleading whine emanated from the shadows and recalled Pixie to rationality. As she realised she had been standing dumbly gaping at Apollo while she thought about him an angry flush crept up her face. In a sudden move, she reached for Hector's leash. 'Look, I don't know what you're doing here but right now I have to take my dog out for a walk.'

Apollo watched her drag…literally *drag*…a tattered-looking and clearly terrified little dog out of the corner to clip it onto a leash and lift it into her arms, where she rubbed her chin over the crown of its head and muttered soothingly to it as if it were a baby.

'I have to talk to you. I'll come with you.'

'I don't want you with me and if you have to talk to me about anything I have to say that accusing me of theft and utterly humiliating me where I work wasn't a good opening.'

'I know how desperate you must be for money. That's why I assumed—'

Pixie spun angrily, her little pearly teeth gripped tightly together. 'That's why it doesn't pay to *assume* anything about someone you don't know!'

'Are you always this argumentative? This ready to take offence?'

'Only around you,' Pixie told him truthfully. 'Look, you can wait here while I'm out. I'll be about fifteen minutes,' she said briskly and walked out of the door.

Two steps along the pavement she couldn't quite believe she had had the nerve. After all, the way he talked he knew about Patrick's gambling debts and the threat against his continuing health. She broke out in a cold sweat just thinking about that reality because she really did love her little brother. Patrick didn't have a bad bone in his body. He had made a mistake. He had tried too hard to be one of the boys when he took up playing cards and instead of stopping the habit when he lost money he had gone on gambling in the foolish belief that he could not continue on a losing streak for ever. By the time he had realised his mistake, he had built up a huge debt. But Patrick was working very hard to try and stay on top of that debt. He was an electrician during the day and a bartender at night.

Apollo had dangled a carrot and that she could have walked away even temporarily from the vaguest possibility of help for Patrick shook Pixie. But *was* Apollo offering to help them? No, that was highly unlikely. Why would he help them? He wasn't the benevolent, sympathetic type. Yet why had he come to the salon in the first place and sought her out personally? And then accused her of theft? Her head aching with pointless conjecture, she sighed. Apollo was very complicated. He was also unreadable and impulsive. There was no way she could guess what he had in mind before he chose to tell her.

Apollo examined the grim little room and vented a curse. Women did not as a rule walk out on him, no, not even briefly. But Pixie was headstrong and defiant. Not exactly submissive wife material, a little voice pointed out in his head but he ignored it. He trailed a finger along the worn paperback books on the shelf above the bed and pulled out one to see what she liked to read. It was informative: a pirate in top boots wielding a sword. A reluctant grin of amusement slashed Apollo's lean, darkly handsome features. Just as a book should never be judged by its cover, neither apparently should Pixie be. She was a closet romantic with a taste for the colourful.

Registering that he was hungry, he dug out his cell phone to order lunch for the two of them.

Walking back into her room, Pixie unclipped Hector's leash and watched her pet race under the bed to hide.

Apollo was sprawled in the room's single armchair, long, muscular, jeans-clad legs spread apart, his black

hair feathering round his lean strong face, accentuating the brilliance of eyes that burned like emerald fire.
'Does your dog always behave like that?' he demanded,
frowning.

'Yes. He's scared of everything but he's most afraid
of men. He was ill-treated,' she murmured wryly. 'So,
tell me why you're here.'

'You're in a bind and I am as well. I think it's possible
that we could work out something that settles both our
problems,' Apollo advanced guardedly.

Her smooth brow indented. 'I don't know what you're
talking about.'

'For starters, I will *pay* you if necessary to keep quiet
about what I am about to tell you because it's highly confidential information,' Apollo volunteered.

Faint colour rose over Pixie's cheekbones. 'I don't need
to be paid to keep your secrets. In spite of what you ap-
pear to think, I'm not that malicious or grasping.'

'No, but you are in need of money and the press put
a high value on stories about me,' Apollo pointed out,
compressing his lips. 'You *could* sell the story.'

'Has that happened to you before? Someone selling a
story about you?' she shot at him with sudden curiosity.

'At least half a dozen times. Employees, exes...' Apollo
leant back into the chair, his strong jaw line taut, dark
stubble highlighting his full sculptured mouth. 'That's
the world I live in. That's why I have a carload of bodyguards follow me everywhere I go.'

Pixie had noticed the sleek and expensive car parked
across the street and a man in a suit leaning against the
bonnet while he talked into an earpiece and her grey
eyes widened in wonderment. 'You don't trust anybody,
do you?'

'I trust Vito. I trusted my father as well but he let me

down many times over the years and not least with the terms of his will.'

Belatedly, Pixie recalled the recent death of his parent and the reference to the older man's will made her suspect that they were finally approaching the crux of the matter that had put Apollo 'in a bind'. It was, however, hard for her to credit that anything could trap Apollo Metraxis in a tight corner. He was a force of nature and very rich. He had choices most people never even got to dream of having and he had always had them.

'I have no idea where you're going with this,' she muttered uncomfortably. 'I can't even begin to imagine any set of circumstances where you and I could somehow settle our…er…problems. Are you asking me for some sort of favour or something?'

'I don't ask people for favours. I *pay* them to do things for me.'

'So there's something that you *think* I could do for you that you'd be willing to pay for…is that right?' Pixie pressed in frustration as a knock sounded on the door.

Apollo sprang upright, all leaping energy and strength, startling her into backing away several steps. He didn't want to get to the point, she registered in wonderment. He was skating along the edge of what he wanted to ask her, reluctant to give her that much information.

And Pixie understood that feeling very well. Trust had never come easily to her either. She loved Holly and her brother and Holly's baby and would have done anything for them. Once won, her loyalty was unshakeable and it had caused her a great deal of pain in recent months that she had had to step back from her friendship with Holly because it was simply impossible to be honest about the reasons why she had been more distant and why she had yet to visit Holly and Vito in Italy. Holly would be determined to help and there was no way Pixie could allow herself to take advantage of Holly's newfound wealth and still look herself in the face. Instead she was dealing with her problems as she always did...*alone*.

She stared in disbelief as a procession of covered dishes were brought in by suited men and piled up on her battered coffee table along with cutlery and napkins and even wine and glasses. 'For goodness' sake, what on earth is all this?' she framed, wide-eyed.

'Lunch,' Apollo explained, whipping off covers as his men trooped back out again. 'I'm starving. Help yourself.'

He whipped off the final cover. 'That's for the dog.'

'The *dog*?' Pixie gasped.

'I like animals, probably more than I like people,' Apollo admitted truthfully.

Pixie lifted the plate of meat and biscuit and sniffed it. It smelled a great deal better than Hector's usual food did and she slid it under the side of the bed. Hector was no slowcoach when it came to tucking in and he began chomping on the offering almost immediately.

'Where did you get the food from?' she asked.

'I think it's from the hotel round the corner. There's not much choice round here.'

Pixie nodded slowly and reached for a plate. Apollo did not live like an ordinary person. He got hungry, he phoned his bodyguards and they fetched a choice of foods at an undoubtedly very stiff price. She helped herself to the fish dish.

'Are you going to tell me what's put you in a bind yet?' she enquired ruefully.

'I can't inherit my father's estate without first getting married,' Apollo breathed in a driven undertone. 'He knew how I felt about marriage. After all, it didn't make him very happy. He was married six times in total. My mother died in childbirth but he had to divorce the five wives that followed her.'

Pixie listened with huge eyes. 'A bit like Henry VIII with his six wives,' she mumbled helplessly.

'My father didn't execute any of his, although had he had the power I suspect he would have exercised the right with at least two of them,' Apollo derided.

'And you're *still* an only child? Why would he try to *force* you to marry?'

'He didn't want the family name to die out.'

'But to prevent that from happening...you'd have to have a child,' Pixie pointed out with a frown.

'Yes. He stitched me up every way there is. My legal team say the will is valid as he was in sound mind when he had it drawn up. I also have a five-year window of opportunity to carry out his wishes and inherit, which is deemed reasonable,' Apollo ground out between gritted white teeth. '*Thee mou*...how can anyone call any of it *reasonable*? It's insane!'

'It's...it's...er...unusual,' Pixie selected uncertainly. 'But I suppose a rich, powerful man like your father thought he had the right to do whatever he liked with his own estate.'

'*Ne*...yes,' Apollo conceded gruffly in Greek. 'But I have been running my father's business empire for many years now and his will feels like a *betrayal*.'

'I can understand that,' Pixie said thoughtfully. 'You trusted him. I used to believe my father when he told me he'd never go back into prison but he didn't even try to go straight and keep his promise. My mother was the same. She said she would stop stealing and she didn't. The only thing that finally stopped her was ill health.'

Apollo studied her in astonishment, not knowing whether or not to be offended that she had compared his much-respected and law-abiding father to a couple of career criminals.

Enjoying her delicious fish, Pixie was deep in thought and surprised that she could relax to that extent in Apollo's volatile radius. 'I get your predicament,' she confided. 'But the terms of the will must be public property, and they aren't confidential, so what—?'

'I have decided that I must meet the terms,' Apollo incised grimly. 'I am not prepared to lose the home and the business empire that three generations of my family built up from nothing.'

'Attachment meets practicality,' Pixie quipped. 'I still don't understand what any of this has to do with me.'

Apollo set down his plate and lifted his wine glass. 'I intend to meet the demands of the will on my *own* terms,' he told her with emphasis, his remarkable green eyes glittering below black curling lashes. 'I don't want a wife. I will hire a woman to marry me and have my child. We will then separate and divorce and my life will return to normal again.'

'And what about the child?' Pixie prompted with a frown of dismay. 'What will happen to the child in all this?'

'The child will remain with its mother and I will attempt to be an occasional father to the best of my ability. My goal is to negotiate a civilised and workable arrangement with the woman of my choice.'

'Well, good luck with that ambition,' Pixie muttered, tucking into her meal with appetite while sitting cross-legged on the floor beside the coffee table because there was only one chair and predictably Apollo had not offered it to her. 'It sounds like a very tall order to me… and anything but practical. What woman wants to marry and have a child and then be divorced?'

'A woman I have paid well to marry and divorce me,' Apollo said drily. 'I don't want to end up with one who will cling.'

Pixie rolled her eyes and laughed. 'When a woman knows she's not wanted, she's rarely clingy.'

'Then you'd be surprised to learn how hard I find it to prise myself free of even the shortest liaison. Women who become accustomed to my lifestyle don't want to give it up.'

Pixie set down her plate and lifted the wine glass he had filled. 'You do indeed have a problem,' she commented with a certain amount of amusement at his predicament. 'But I really don't understand why you're confiding in me of all people!'

'Are you always this slow on the uptake?'

Her smooth brow indented as she sipped her wine and looked up at him enquiringly from below her spidery lashes. 'What do you mean?'

She had beautiful eyes, Apollo acknowledged in surprise, eyes of a luminous clear grey that shone like polished silver in certain lights. 'What do you think I'm doing here with you?' he prompted huskily.

Green eyes met bemused grey and an arrow of forbidden heat shot to the heart of Pixie. She froze into uneasy stillness, her heart banging inside her chest like a panic button that had been stabbed because all of a sudden she felt vulnerable...vulnerable and...*needy*, the very worst word in her vocabulary when it related to a man.

'I believe that for the right price *you* could be the woman I marry and divorce,' Apollo spelt out smoothly. 'I would get a wife, who knows and accepts that the marriage is a temporary arrangement, and you would get your brother off the hook and a much more comfortable and secure life afterwards.'

As Pixie's throat convulsed, her wine went down the wrong way and she set the glass down on the low table with a jarring snap as she went off into a coughing, choking fit. He was thinking of her? *Her?* Her and him, the ultimate mismatch? The woman he had accused of being a thief? Was he certifiably insane? Or simply madly eccentric?

CHAPTER THREE

SPLUTTERING AND GASPING for breath, Pixie waved a silencing hand and rushed out of her room to the bathroom. There she got control of the coughing and rinsed her mouth with water taken from her cupped hand. In the mirror over the sink she saw her sad, watering panda eyes and groaned out loud. She looked dreadful. Her eyeliner was rubbed all round her eyes and there was even a smear across one cheek. She did her best with what little there was in the bathroom to tidy herself up.

Apollo Metraxis was offering to rescue Patrick from the debts he was drowning in if she married him in a pretend marriage. *And* had a child with him. *Don't forget the child,* she told herself while she clutched the sink to keep herself upright. She was blown away entirely by the crazy prospect of having a child with Apollo, having sex with Apollo... Swallowing hard, she breathed in deep. It was the most insane idea she had ever heard and she couldn't work out how or why he had decided to approach her with it.

Was he nuts? Temporarily off his rocker after the death of his father? Grounded again, she returned to her room and stared at him.

'That has to be the most ridiculous idea I've ever heard and I can't believe you're serious. I mean...' Pixie paused '...you don't even know me.'

'I'm not suggesting a normal marriage. I know what I need to know about you.'

'Little more than an hour ago you accused me of stealing your wallet!' Pixie fired back at him unimpressed.

'Because I know how desperate you have to be for money. You know that if your brother fails to make a payment or doesn't pay what he's supposed to pay his life could be on the line. He owes that money to a thug, who rules with fear and intimidation,' Apollo countered levelly. 'He could choose to make an example of your brother to deter others from making the same mistake.'

Apollo did indeed know exactly how precarious her brother's position was. Her tummy churned sickly at his confirmation that Patrick's creditor was a violent man because regardless of the beating Patrick had received she had hoped that that was the worst that would be done to him. She paled. 'But that still doesn't explain why you would approach someone like me!' she gasped.

'I told you that I prefer to choose a woman I can pay to marry me. I also want to be in control of the whole arrangement and the way I would set this up would mean that you *had* to follow the rules until our arrangement ends. That feels safer to me. It wouldn't be in your interests or your brother's to cross me or to admit to anyone that our marriage was phony,' he pointed out with assurance. 'Were you to admit that to the wrong person I could be challenged in a courtroom and I could lose my father's estate for ever. If you did betray me, you would be breaking the terms of our agreement and you would land you and your brother straight back into the same trouble that you're in right now.'

It was quite a speech, a sobering and intimidating speech that told her a lot she would rather not have known about exactly how Apollo's mind worked. He wanted a woman over whom he had total control, a woman who had to strictly adhere to his conditions or lose all benefits from the arrangement.

'I hear what you're saying,' Pixie breathed tautly, 'but I think it's twisted. You want a wife you can blackmail into doing what you want her to do, someone powerless. I could not be that woman.'

'Oh, don't underestimate yourself. I think you're gutsy enough to take me on,' Apollo told her with grudging amusement in his gaze. 'Did you or did you not grasp the fact that I am offering to save you and your brother from the consequences of his stupidity?'

Pixie reddened. Silence fell. In the interim, Apollo made use of his cell phone and spoke in what she assumed was rapid Greek.

'You're serious about this…?' she almost whispered in sheer bewilderment. 'But you said you need to have a child as well, and—'

'If you fail to conceive the marriage would end in divorce within eighteen months. I can't afford to waste more time than that,' Apollo imparted without hesitation. 'However, you would still get the same financial payoff. In that way, whether you have a child or not, you would still benefit from a debt-free future. '

A knock came on the door again. This time it was Pixie who rushed to answer it because she desperately needed a breathing space to get her thoughts in order and was thinking of diving for the bathroom again. Two men entered and deftly cleared away the dishes, leaving behind only the wine and the glasses.

'There's no way on earth I could go to bed with you!' Pixie spluttered out bluntly without meaning to as soon as the door had shut on the men's exit.

Apollo studied her in open astonishment and then he

flung his handsome dark head back and roared with un-
fettered amusement. In fact he laughed so hard he almost
tipped the chair back while she stared at him in disbelief.

'I really don't understand how you can find that so
funny,' Pixie snapped when he had regained control
of himself. 'You're talking about me having sex with a
stranger and that may be something you do on a fairly
regular basis but it's not something I would do! You're
also talking about having an awful lot of sex,' she told
him half an octave higher, her voice thinning with extreme stress and embarrassment. 'Because it could take
months and months to conceive a child. I couldn't do
it. There's absolutely no way I could do that with you!'

'You sound a little hysterical and I'm surprised,'
Apollo admitted. 'Holly's the starry-eyed type but you
struck me as more sensible. Marry me and try to have
a child and you won't be struggling in a dump like this
to save your brother and make a decent life. All the bad
things will go away... I can make that happen. You won't
get a better offer.'

Mortification had claimed Pixie because she knew she
had sounded panic-stricken. Face hot, she retreated to the
bed and sank down on the edge of the mattress. In truth
the thought of having sex with Apollo drove every sensible thought from her mind and only provoked a giant
'no' from every corner of her being. A long, *long* time
ago she had promised herself that sex would only ever
be combined with love in her life. She hadn't saved her
virginity simply to throw it away in some immoral arrangement with Apollo Metraxis intended to conceive a
child and moreover a child he didn't *really* want.

Apollo studied her in frustration. He didn't understand
what was wrong. A woman had never found him unattractive before. He knew she didn't like him but he didn't

consider liking necessary to a successful sexual liaison. Sex was like food in Apollo's life, something he enjoyed on a frequent basis and wasted little time thinking about. He was amazed that she had concentrated her objections on the need for a sexual relationship. Head down bent, she sat on the side of the bed in a rigid position with one arm stretched down in an unavailing attempt to lure the terrified dog out from underneath the bed. But the dog was too wary of Apollo's presence to emerge. He could see its beady little eyes gleaming watchfully from deep under the mattress.

'Tell me what the problem is...' he invited impatiently.

'I don't want to have a baby with someone who doesn't love me or my child,' Pixie muttered in a rush. 'That's way too like what I had growing up with the parents from hell!'

Apollo was taken aback. 'I don't want a woman who loves me because she might well want to stay married to me and I will want my freedom back as soon as I have fulfilled the terms of the will. Rejecting a wife who loved me could well lead to her breaking our agreement and telling someone that the marriage was a fake created to circumvent the will and allow me to inherit. And speaking for myself, I can't put love on the table for *any* woman. But, I *would* hope and expect to love my child.'

That admission soothed only one of Pixie's concerns because her brain could not surmount the unimaginable challenge of going to bed with Apollo again and again and *again*. A trickle of heat sidled through her slender frame as she lifted her head a few inches higher and focussed on her tormentor. He was gorgeous and he knew it but that did not mean he would be kind or considerate in bed. What did she feel like? A medieval maiden being auctioned off for a good price? That was nonsense because the choice, the decision was hers alone. And women had been marrying men for reasons far removed from love for centuries. Some women married to have children, some for money, some for security and some to please their families. She was making too much of a fuss over the sexual component. Sex was a physical pastime, not a mental one.

So, did that mean that she was actually considering Apollo's ridiculous proposition? She took a mental look at her life as it was. She was drowning in her brother's debt. She didn't have a life. She couldn't *afford* to have a life. She went to work, she came home, ate as cheaply as she could and saved every possible penny. Aside from Hector, whom she adored, it was a pretty miserable life for a young woman but sixth sense warned her that Apollo, if displeased, probably had the power to make even the life of a rich wife a great deal *more* miserable. Even so, when Holly visited the UK, Pixie went to meet her and they would have a meal and a couple of drinks and for a few sunny hours Pixie would forget her worries and enjoy being with her friend again. If she married Apollo, she would surely see much more of Holly, wouldn't she?

But then nothing could make marrying Apollo for money the right or decent thing to do, she reasoned unhappily. It would be akin to renting out her womb. And although she loved children and very much missed her friend Holly's adorable son, Angelo, from when they had both lived with her, she had never planned to have a child so young or to raise one alone. To plan to do that would be wrong, she thought with a shudder of distaste. And Apollo had also reminded her that circumventing his father's will would be breaking the law and she refused to be involved in anything of that nature.

'I can't believe you are willing to go to such lengths

just for money…but then I've never had enough money to miss,' Pixie admitted wryly. 'I guess it's different for you.'

'I'm already a very rich man in my own right,' Apollo contradicted drily. 'But there is more to this than money. There is my family home on the island where all my relatives are buried. There are the businesses originally founded by my grandfather and my great-grandfather, the very roots of my family. It took my father's death for me to appreciate that I'm much more attached to those roots than I was ever willing to admit even to myself.'

His obvious sincerity disconcerted Pixie. She understood that he had taken those things for granted until he was forced to confront the threat of losing them.

'Lying and pretending wouldn't come naturally to me,' she told him flatly. 'And faking the marriage would also be breaking the law, which I couldn't do. I don't even have a traffic violation on my record,' she told him truthfully. 'Because of my experiences growing up I won't do anything that breaks the law.'

'But we would be faithfully following the terms of the will, which specifies that I must marry and produce a child—boy or girl—within the space of five years. My intent to eventually go for a divorce is not barred by the will. If the marriage is consummated and we have a child it will be, to all intents and purposes, a *normal* legal marriage,' Apollo told her forcefully.

Pixie hovered, her small heart-shaped face pale and stiff. 'I don't want to be involved. I realise that you think I'm an easy mark but I couldn't do it. I won't discuss this with anyone either. I should think anyone I told would threaten to lock me up and throw away the key because they'd think I was crazy!'

Apollo rose slowly to his feet, dominating the room

with his height and breadth. 'You're not thinking this through.' Reaching into his pocket, he withdrew a card and set it down on the table. 'My private number if you change your mind.'

'I'm not going to change my mind,' Pixie told him stonily.

Apollo said nothing. He paused at the door, looking at that soft ripe mouth of hers, his body hardening in response to the imagery flashing through his inventive mind. 'It would've been good in bed. I find you surprisingly attractive.'

'Can't say the same,' Pixie retorted as she yanked open the door with a shaking hand. 'I don't like you. You're arrogant and insensitive and completely ruthless when it comes to getting what you want.'

'But I still make you hot, which infuriates you,' Apollo murmured huskily. 'You're not very good at faking disinterest.'

Her grey eyes sparkled with anger. 'You're not irresistible, Apollo!'

He lifted a lean-fingered hand and tilted up her chin. 'Are you sure of that?' he asked thickly, a Greek accent he rarely revealed roughening and lowering his dark drawl to a pitch that vibrated like a storm warning down her stiff spine.

'One hundred per cent certain,' she was mumbling as his breath fanned her cheek and the scent of him flared her nostrils and her mouth ran dry while her heartbeat raced into the danger zone.

'I bet I could get you to break the law,' Apollo murmured soft and low, all untamed masculinity and dominance. 'I bet I could get you to do just about anything I wanted you to. I even bet that I could make you *enjoy* breaking the rules...'

Her knees were trembling, her feet welded to the floor by the mesmeric effect of those stunning green eyes firing down into her own. 'You'd like to think so.'

Her pupils were fully dilated, her breathing was audible. Her nipples were making tiny indentations in her top and Apollo was hard as a rock. He bent his head a fraction more and traced her stubborn little mouth with his. She jerked almost off balance and his arms snapped round her to steady her. She couldn't breathe then for excitement. It was the most extraordinary sensation. Suddenly she wanted what she hadn't wanted until that moment. She wanted to stretch up on tiptoe and claim the kiss he had teased her with and refused to give.

Apollo bit out a laugh, perceptive eyes mocking her. 'Stubborn and proud. That's dangerous in my vicinity because I'm stubborn and proud as hell too. We'd clash but we'd also have fireworks, not something I usually look for with a woman but I'd make an exception for you, *koukla mou*. I would enjoy making you eat every word of your defiance and your denial...'

Her blood ran cold in her veins because she believed him. Below the bed Hector uttered a soft little growl that she had never heard from him before.

Apollo laughed again with genuine appreciation. 'Aw, stop kidding yourself, dog! You're not going to attack. You're too scared even to come out from under the bed. What do you call him?' he asked, disconcerting her with that sudden change of subject.

'Hector.'

'Hector was a Trojan prince and a great army commander in Greek mythology. Did you know that?' he enquired lazily as he strolled out of the door.

'No, I didn't. I just thought the name suited him,' she mumbled weakly.

She didn't breathe again until she had closed the door and she rested back against it with eyes shut and the strangest sense of disappointment filtering through her. In the most disturbing way Apollo Metraxis had energised her. The threat gone, Hector scampered joyously out from below the bed and danced at her feet. She lifted him up, stroking what remained of his ragged little ears, and cuddled him. 'A Trojan prince, not just an ordinary dog, Hector. I named you well,' she whispered, burying her face in his tousled fur, feeling her lips tingle as she thought of that almost-but-not-quite kiss that had left her foolishly, mindlessly craving more.

Patrick Skyped her that evening, his thin face worn, eyes shadowed. 'I've got bad news,' he told her heavily. 'Maria's pregnant and she's not well.'

'Pregnant?' Pixie gasped in dismay.

Patrick grimaced. 'It wasn't planned but we want the baby. We've been together three years now,' he reminded his sister with a weak attempt at a smile. 'I just wish the pregnancy wasn't making her so ill because she can't stand on her feet all day in a shop in her current condition. I'm never here, I'm always working...who's going to look after her?'

'Give her my congratulations,' Pixie urged, concealing her feelings because she very well knew that her brother's pregnant partner could bring his entire debt repayment scheme tumbling down round their ears because it was a struggle for him to make his monthly payment as it was.

Her brother's blue eyes glittered. 'I hate asking but could you manage anything extra this month?'

'I'll see what I can do,' Pixie said thickly, not wanting him to realise that she could see the tears in his eyes.

A few minutes later the call was complete and Pixie felt as though she had received a punch in the stomach.

Patrick and Maria's financial situation was as fragile as a house built of cards. If one card fell, they would all fall. She groaned out loud. She couldn't afford to give Patrick any more money and she should have admitted that upfront. Unfortunately her panic-induced thoughts had flown straight to Apollo because she wanted her little brother to stay alive and in one piece and if he couldn't keep up those payments, he could well pay with his life.

Patrick was under threat and now there was Maria and a new baby on the way to consider as well, Pixie reflected wretchedly. How could she ignore their plight? How could she turn her back on them when Apollo had made it clear that if she did as he asked he would make all the bad things go away? And suddenly she was just desperate for those bad things to go away and for life to return to normal again.

Apollo as saviour? That concept didn't work. Apollo was more into helping himself than other people. In fact Pixie and her brother were more like chess pieces to be moved strategically on Apollo's master board. The human cost, the rights and wrongs and emotions didn't come into it for Apollo and how much simpler that must make his life, she thought enviously. She lifted the card and snatched up her phone.

I will be your Baby Mama if you settle my brother's debts, she texted with a sinking heart.

Ideals, she was learning, wouldn't be any comfort if her brother or Maria or the baby got hurt or were left alone in the world. Apollo had found her price and she felt humiliated, and even worse manipulated, for he had made her crave his mouth that afternoon and the memory of that unnerved her. It was one thing to defy Apollo, another thing entirely to contemplate being married to him and wholly within his power.

You won't regret it. We'll talk business the next time we meet.

Business, *not* marriage, she reflected uneasily, but maybe that was the right way to look at it, as an arrangement rather than a relationship. As a deal between two people rather than the intimacy normal between a married couple. He wouldn't really be her husband and she wouldn't really be his wife. Mostly they would be faking it…wouldn't they? Would that make it easier to bear?

CHAPTER FOUR

'IT'S QUITE SIMPLE,' Apollo murmured in a cold, dangerous tone. 'You pack up you and your dog and you'll be
picked up this evening.'

'I can't just walk out on my job, and I'm supposed to
give notice when I move out.'

'My staff will organise everything of that nature for
you. You don't need to worry. I want you in London with
me tonight, so that we can get on with the preparations.'

'What preparations?'

'You'll have to sign legal papers, see a doctor, buy
clothes. There must be a dozen entries on the to-do list
I've had drawn up for you. You're going to be very busy.'

Pixie thought about her brother and briefly closed her
eyes, digging deep for composure. She had just put her
life and her free will in Apollo's hands and the pressure
was on *her* now. 'Where will I be staying?'

'At my apartment. It'll be more discreet than a hotel
would be and I won't be there for most of the week. I'll
be working in Athens.'

'OK.' Pixie forced herself to agree because she knew it
was only the first step in another hundred or more steps
when she would have to obediently fall in with Apollo's
wishes. Dear heaven, had she ever hated a man so much?

Vito was one of the very few men Pixie had learned

to trust. She could see his love for her friend, Holly, every time he looked at his wife and his feelings for his son were equally obvious. But Pixie had had few such role models while she was growing up. Her own father had frequently resorted to domestic violence when he was drunk. He had beaten her mother and Pixie as well, calling her 'a mouthy little cow' for trying to interfere. When he wasn't in prison serving time for his burglaries, he had often taken his bad moods out on his family. Pixie had never had Holly's cosy, idealistic images of family life because she had experienced family life in the raw. Her father had married her mother when she fell pregnant but she had never seen any love or affection between them. Patrick had been born within a year of his sister's birth and her mother had found it a challenge to cope with two young kids.

By the time Pixie was eight years old, both children had been placed in a council run children's home because her mother had finally been imprisoned for her incessant shoplifting. Social workers had taken a very dim view of a mother trying to teach her children to steal. The council home and the various foster homes that followed had occasionally contained men with sexual designs on their charges. Pixie had been very young when she first learned to fear the opposite sex and the fact that she went on looking like a much younger child due to her lack of adolescent development had ensured that she had to remain on her guard around such men for years longer than most.

The foster home that had become the first real *home* for Pixie had been Sylvia and Maurice Ware's and she had gone to them when she was twelve. The semi-retired farmer and his wife had had a spacious farmhouse in the Devonshire countryside and they had been devoted guardians to the often traumatised children who had come to live with them. Now Maurice was dead, the farmhouse sold and Sylvia lived in sheltered accommodation but Pixie had never forgotten the debt she owed to the older couple for the love, kindness and understanding they had shown her. And it was in their home that she had met Holly and their friendship had been forged, even though Pixie was eighteen months younger.

Her possessions fitted into her one suitcase and a box she begged off the local corner shop. She left an apologetic message on her employer Sally's answering machine. What else could she do with Apollo calling all the shots? But being forced into such dangerous life changes genuinely frightened her. What would she do if Apollo decided that she wasn't suitable to be his wife after all? Where would she go? How would she find another job? She didn't trust Apollo and she didn't want to end up on the street, homeless and unemployed, particularly not with Hector to worry about.

A limousine arrived to collect her. The driver came to the door and carried out her luggage and then produced a pet carrier, which Hector refused to enter. Pixie protested and promised that the little dog would be quiet and well-behaved if he was allowed to travel on her lap. She climbed into the opulent car with an engulfing sense of detached disbelief. She'd had glimpses of Holly and Vito's wealth, had attended their wedding, had seen impressive photos of their Italian home, but Holly didn't wear much jewellery or particularly fancy clothes and, essentially, she hadn't *changed*. It was surprisingly easy to meet up with Holly and forget that she was the wife of a very rich man.

The luxurious interior of the limousine fascinated Pixie. It had a television and a phone and a bar. It was a long drive but there were regular stops to exercise Hector and an evening meal stop for Pixie at a very swanky hotel. It was only there that she noticed another car was accompanying them because it was one of the men in it who escorted her into the fancy dining room and urged her to choose whatever she liked from the menu. Pixie was so horrified by the prices on the menu and so scared that the bill would be handed to her at the end of the meal that even though she was starving she only dared to have soup, which came with a roll. Of course no one presented her with a bill. The big beefy bodyguard or whatever he was appeared to be there to take care of such necessities while Hector waited in the car.

By the time they finally arrived in London, Pixie was exhausted and living on her nerves. It was after ten in the evening and it was dark and, with Hector cradled in her arms, she left the limo in the underground car park and walked into a lift with the big beefy guy and his mate towering over her.

'What're your names?' she asked nervously.

'Theo and Dmitri, Miss Robinson. You're not really supposed to notice us,' Theo told her gently. 'We're here to take care of you but we're staff.'

It was yet another strong message that Apollo lived in a different world because Pixie could not imagine ever ignoring anyone in such a way. But at that moment she reminded herself that she had more pressing concerns. Would she see Apollo this evening? The lift stopped directly into a massive apartment foyer and she realised that it had to be a private lift only used by him and his employees.

A small, portly older man in a jacket approached her. 'I'm Manfred, Miss Robinson. I look after the apartment. Let me show you to your room.'

Pixie followed him across the foyer towards a corridor and on the way past saw into a large reception room where she glimpsed a lithe blonde beauty standing talking with a drink in her hand. One of Apollo's women? Probably, she thought. He always seemed to have a woman on the go. She would have to ask him what he planned to do after their marriage if they got that far because no way was she prepared to sleep with a man sleeping with other women at the same time. That wasn't negotiable yet the picture of a quiet, clean-living version of Apollo married refused to gel.

'This is the garden room,' Manfred announced grandly, walking across a big, lushly appointed bedroom to indicate the patio doors. He buzzed them open to show her the outside space. 'Perfect for the little dog...'

'Yes,' Pixie agreed in wonderment. Stepping out, she noticed that part of the roof garden was neatly and clearly temporarily fenced off, presumably to prevent Hector straying into the glimmering blue pool that lay beyond it.

'Can I get you any refreshments?' he asked cheerfully.

'I wouldn't say no to some sandwiches,' Pixie muttered apologetically.

Pixie unpacked while Hector explored the new environment and his own first private outside space. In one corner of the room sat a fur-lined pet bed with a roof. Hector sniffed all round it, finally decided it wasn't actively unfriendly and got into it. Manfred brought tea and sandwiches on a tray. Pixie went for a shower in the lovely bathroom, bemused to find herself dropped in the midst of such extreme comfort and luxury. Comfy in her shortie pyjamas, she curled up on the bed with her supper and ate.

Apollo had already told Lauren that he had an early start in the morning and that her uninvited visit was inconvenient. He had given her wine, made the kind of meaning-less chit-chat that bored him and sidestepped a blatantly obvious invitation to have sex. He never brought his lov-ers back to his various properties. He took them to a hotel or went to their place because that meant that he could leave whenever he liked.

'You want me to leave, don't you?' Lauren said in a whiny little-girl voice that set his teeth on edge.

'Tonight doesn't suit me,' Apollo pointed out with-out apology. 'I have a busy schedule and I also have a guest staying.'

'Another woman?' she gasped.

And that was it for Apollo. Lauren had been in his life exactly two days. He hadn't yet slept with her and now he knew he never would because her attitude turned him off. Lauren stalked out in a snit, leaving Apollo free to indulge in his desire to see Pixie. Of course he wanted to see her, he reasoned with himself while his brain ques-tioned *why* he would want to see her. But Pixie was very probably the woman he was going to marry and there-fore infinitely more important than a casual hook-up like Lauren. And in any case he wanted to see if Hector liked his new hideaway bed.

With a brief knock on Pixie's bedroom door, Apollo opened it.

He was just in time to catch the look of fear on Pixie's face and the way she slammed back apprehensively against the headboard. 'Sorry, did I startle you?' he said, knowing that 'startled' didn't come near to covering her excessive reaction and wondering what had caused it.

Pale, Pixie suddenly reddened and unglued her spine from the headboard to straighten her narrow shoulders. 'It's all right,' she said with forced casualness. 'I thought you were entertaining?'

'No.' Apollo stared at her. She was wearing pyjamas and there was nothing elegant or alluring about them but, while his rational mind was telling him that, his body was reacting as if she were half naked. The nipples of her small breasts pushed against the thin cotton and her slender crossed legs were exposed yet he only had to look into her flushed and ridiculously appealing face and that bee-stung mouth and he was throbbing, grateful for the suit jacket he still wore as a cover.

'Well, I'm here,' Pixie pointed out nervously. 'Thanks for the bed for Hector.'

Apollo glanced at Hector, who had made himself as small and unnoticeable as possible at the back of the big bed, and a slanting, almost boyish grin flashed across his lean, strong face without warning. 'I thought he might as well hide in comfort.'

He looked amazing when he smiled like that, Pixie ruminated. She hadn't known he could smile like that or that he was a soft touch when it came to dogs, but he so obviously had not been joking when he said he often preferred animals to people. It gave him a more human side, made her a touch less unnerved by him. As for those dazzling, unexpectedly green eyes illuminating his hard dark features, it was a challenge to look away from them. But then of course he had appeal. He was a real player. Young, hot and rich, he was a target for hungry, ambitious and designing women, which was probably why he didn't like women very much. At least that was what she had privately decided about him even though she didn't know if it was true. And why should she care? Why was she even thinking about him in such a way? What Apollo Metraxis was really like shouldn't matter to her, should it?

And the need to stick to business belatedly impressed

her as a very good attitude to take because she did not want to be getting curious about Apollo and wondering what made him tick. Nor did she want to be admiring his stunning male beauty. None of that should matter to her, she told herself urgently.

'Do you mind telling me what you intend to do about my brother's debt?' she pressed tightly.

'If we go ahead and marry he can forget about it because I'll take care of it. If we stay married and you meet my conditions—'

'Getting pregnant?' she interrupted in dismay.

'No, that won't be on the table because it would be unreasonable. You may not conceive and if you don't I can hardly punish you for not doing so,' he conceded. 'As long as you try. That and confidentiality are really all I'm expecting from you. Whether we're successful or otherwise that debt will not come back to haunt your brother.'

'You're paying it off?'

'No, I'm taking over the payments,' Apollo lied without skipping a beat. 'Look on it as my method of ensuring you keep to your side of the bargain throughout our association.'

'It's not necessary to put that kind of pressure on me. I keep my promises,' Pixie argued, unhappy with what he was telling her.

'My tactics work,' Apollo countered levelly, feeling an unexpected stab of discomfiture for not telling her the truth, and the truth was that he already owned the debt in its entirety. After all, there was no way he could have entertained any kind of ongoing arrangement with a thug running an illegal gambling den.

Pixie swallowed hard on the angry, defiant response she wanted to make. When it came to the gambling debt, what he was offering was still much better than anything she could have hoped to achieve on her own. It would take the financial stress off Patrick and his partner and allow them to get on with their lives and concentrate on their coming baby. On the other hand Apollo's decision to maintain the 'carrot and stick' approach towards their marriage would put the weight of expectation squarely on Pixie's shoulders instead and it would worry her constantly that in some field she would fail to please and her loss of freedom and self-will would end up being worthless.

'I think that if you're prepared to marry me, you could be a little more trusting.'

'How can you say that? When I walked in you looked at me as though you expected me to attack you!' Apollo grated in condemnation. 'You don't trust me either.'

'It's nothing personal. I don't trust men generally.' Pixie lifted her chin. 'And why do I have to see a doctor?'

'Health check. Obviously there's no point in us marrying if it turns out that you may not be able to conceive.'

'So, presumably,' Pixie framed, 'you're being tested as well?'

'No.'

'Forty per cent of infertility problems are *male*,' Pixie pointed out. 'Not much point getting me tested if you're not going to get tested too.'

Apollo hadn't thought of that angle and for some inexplicable reason he realised that the suggestion that he might not be fertile really annoyed him. He opened the door. 'I'll see you tomorrow. By the way, *wear* the outfit I had put in the wardrobe for you.'

'Outfit?' she gasped, sliding off the bed and opening the wardrobe to see the blue dress and jacket that hung there in a garment bag and the silvery designer shoes and bag stowed beneath. 'What gives you the idea that you can tell me what to wear?'

'It's another milestone on the road to becoming my wife. Naturally I want you to look your best,' Apollo fielded, dragging his glittering gaze from his perusal of her slender thighs to jerk open the bedroom door again. Maybe he should've taken Lauren to bed, he reflected in annoyance, because he was deeply uneasy about the strength of Pixie's appeal. *Thee mou,* what was the matter with him? She wasn't a beauty but she was exceptionally pretty and there was something remarkably sexy about her as well, something that drew him on a level he didn't understand. Was it her expressive face? Those interestingly perky breasts? The tight bottom? The so touchable thighs and small, slender feet?

Did he feel sorry for her? Was that the source of her strange appeal? He didn't require a therapist to tell him that she suffered from low self-esteem. In the act of shutting the door, he turned and caught the filthy look she was shooting him while thinking herself unobserved and he strode down the corridor to his own bedroom laughing and feeling surprisingly upbeat for the first time since his father's death. No, he didn't feel sorry for Pixie, he *liked* that gutsy irreverent streak of hers even though he was out of necessity being forced to ensure that she reined it in. She really wasn't impressed by him. Or by his wealth. And when had he ever met with that attitude before in a woman? In truth it was a real first for him. The women he was accustomed to would have snatched the outfit out to check that it was designer and would then have praised his generosity with loads of gratitude and flattery to ensure that he did it again.

Pixie? *Not impressed.* Apollo grinned.

* * *

Pixie woke at seven to be greeted by Manfred drawing back the curtains and setting her breakfast down on a table by the window and stepping out through the patio doors to set down a dog dish for Hector. 'Mr Metraxis asks that you be ready for nine,' he told her quietly.

Pixie breakfasted like a king. She loved her food and had always had a healthy appetite. Staying in Apollo's palatial apartment was even better, she imagined, than staying in an exclusive hotel. After a shower, she dried her hair and took special care with her make-up before getting dressed.

She walked uncertainly into the huge main reception room and Apollo stared.

'Turn round,' he told her thickly, turning his fingers to emphasise the order.

Apollo was rapt. She was so incredibly dainty and feminine in that blue dress with the high heels accentuating her delicate ankles that he wanted to lift her off her feet and spin her round, and it was a weird prompting that bewildered him. She had the figure a model would kill for without the height.

'I like the dress,' he said, which wasn't surprising since he had personally selected it.

'It's elegant but I'm not used to wearing skirts or heels,' she complained. 'I'm more of a tomboy than a fashion queen.'

He took her to see a private gynaecologist. She was questioned, examined and scanned and blood tests were taken. The results would be in by the following morning. As she emerged she saw Apollo standing talking urgently into his phone. 'Did you have any idea? Well, no, I didn't think it through either...it's *not* funny, Vito. It was gross.'

Apollo finished the call and strode towards her with

all the eagerness of a male who could not get out of the plush surgery fast enough. 'Ready to go?'

Pixie was trying not to laugh because he had honestly sounded so shocked by what being tested had entailed and she thought it served him right after the process she had undergone without complaint. Evidently he did listen occasionally to a voice other than his own and he was playing fair at least.

'Where to now?' she prompted.

'My lawyers, after which you go shopping.'

'Oh? For what?'

'For a wedding dress obviously and all the rest of it. I'm putting you in the charge of a professional buyer and fashion stylist. She knows what you need as per my instructions. All you have to do is act like a mannequin.'

'But you haven't got the test results back yet.'

'Think positive...' Apollo bent down, his stubbled jaw line grazing her cheek a tiny bit, and every nerve in her body tightened like a string pulled taut. 'And I saw you smiling when you heard me talking to Vito,' he murmured huskily. 'No, I didn't enjoy being handed a porn mag but *ne*...yes, I had a fantasy and it was about you.'

As Apollo pressed her back into the limo, Pixie twisted her head back to gape at him. *'Me?'* she repeated in disbelief.

Green eyes roamed over her burning face with dark satisfaction. 'You, *koukla mou.*'

Luminous eyes taking on a faint bluish cast from the dress she wore, Pixie stared at him in astonishment. 'You're kidding?'

'Why would I be kidding? If I couldn't be attracted to you, how could we do this?'

It was a fair point but the idea that Apollo, all rippling male-muscle perfection and stunningly beautiful, could consider her attractive still stupefied Pixie. And while she stared, frozen to her seat, Apollo moved, scooping her off the seat and settling her down into his lap at a speed that thoroughly unnerved her. But then his mouth traced very gently over hers and that instinctive kick of fear that generally made her back away from men was soothed by that subtle approach, which seemed ridiculously unthreatening. Of course, it didn't dawn on her just at that moment that Apollo had an unequalled sensual skill set that allowed him to read women very easily.

The tip of his tongue traced her upper lip and something deep down inside just melted in Pixie. He followed that tactic up with a nibble at her full lower lip and she shivered, her whole body prickling with awareness to an almost painful degree. No man had ever made her feel anything like that before and she found it wildly seductive not to feel afraid. He teased her lips open and darted his tongue in lightly and a ball of erotic heat exploded in her pelvis and one of her hands flew up into his hair, feathering through the luxuriant strands to cup his well-shaped skull. She felt hot all over and curiously energised, almost as if someone had told her she could fly when all her life she had felt grounded and awkward.

His mouth was hard and yet his lips were soft and she was exploring every sensation with her brain and her body. He tasted so good, like water after a drought, like food after a famine. His mouth claimed hers with increasing pressure and her breasts ached inside her bra, liquid heat pushing between her thighs.

He was so warm she wanted to press into his lean, muscular frame and somehow meld with him. He framed her face with his hands and kissed her with steadily escalating passion and the hungry demand she recognised was thrilling rather than scary. She tipped her head back, allowing him all the access he wanted, jerking at each erotic plunge of his tongue and on fire for the next, which was why it was such a shock when without the smallest warning his hands dropped to her waist and he propelled her back into the seat he had snatched her off.

Blinking with disconcertion and sensual intoxication, Pixie looked at him with a frown of incomprehension as to why he had so abruptly stopped.

'For such a small woman you pack a hell of a punch!' Apollo growled accusingly, because he had been within an inch of ripping off her panties and bringing her down on his aching body, satisfying the raw need that had come at him out of nowhere. And he didn't like it, he didn't like it one bit because he had never been that close to losing control with a woman since he was a teen, and remembering that time when he had been little more than a boy toy for a mature woman's gratification brought him out in a cold sweat of revulsion.

'It was only a kiss,' she framed shakily between tingling lips, even though her body was telling her different and reacting in all sorts of disappointed ways to that sudden severance from his.

'I was ready to have you right here, right now!' Apollo grated through clenched white teeth, his jaw line rigid because he was so furious that for a few wildly exciting moments he had forgotten who he was and who she was and that the very last thing he had been thinking of was the bottom line.

And the bottom line was business, he reminded himself grimly, the business of satisfying his father's will and making the best he could out of being blackmailed into marriage and fatherhood.

'Here in the car?' Pixie gasped, looking ridiculously shocked by the concept. 'Would you have done that?'

And the very slight widening of his gorgeous green eyes fringed by those outrageously lush black lashes of his told her that he would have and indeed had probably had sex in a limo before. That brought her down to earth again with a timely thump. She was a virgin and he was a man whore and of course he had greater expectations and fewer boundaries than the average person. She wondered how often a first kiss had led into full sex for him and a shudder of distaste rippled through her, chasing off the last of the sexual heat he had evoked.

Aware that he had overreacted and exposed a certain sensitivity he had never ever exposed to anyone before, particularly not a woman, Apollo forced himself to shrug a careless shoulder. 'I suspect that you're likely to find living with me rather shocking. I like sex and I like a lot of it. Considering our current situation it's very positive that we light a fire together.'

Pixie shifted almost imperceptibly away from him to widen the gap between them. *I like sex and I like a lot of it.* It was quite an intimidating announcement for an inexperienced woman to absorb. Pixie's biggest secret, kept even from Holly, was that she had never actually *wanted* a man before. She had always been too wary around men to shake off that inhibition by the time she grew up. Usually the minute a man started touching her she wanted him to stop and feared how far he would try to go. But somehow that instinctive recoil, that fear, had been absent with Apollo and that worried her even while she told herself that it was just as well because there was no way on earth that she could somehow avoid consummating a marriage in which she had to try and conceive a child.

They arrived at a very fancy modern glass office building and, before they got out of the limo, Apollo turned to her to say, 'To all intents and purposes this has to seem like we're planning a normal marriage,' he warned her. 'You must *not* mention your brother's debt or anything of that nature.'

'OK,' Pixie muttered uncertainly.

'All you have to sign is a pre-nuptial agreement with a confidentiality clause included,' he revealed. 'You will have your own legal team to advise you.'

'My...*own*?' she whispered shakily, her eyes wide.

'To advise you of your best interests. You must've had access to legal advice to make the agreement stand up in court,' he explained. 'I know a lot about the subject because every one of my father's wives signed one of these agreements and half of them tried to wriggle out of it during the divorce negotiations.'

'I won't be wriggling anywhere,' Pixie mumbled.

'So, act like a girlfriend, not someone I hired!' Apollo advised in a warning aside.

'How would a girlfriend behave?' she whispered.

'I don't know. I've never had one, only sexual partners,' Apollo admitted, grasping her hand to urge her out of the limo.

'Never?' Pixie repeated incredulously.

'Just think about how a real bride-to-be would behave for this and behave accordingly.'

And an hour later, seated at a large conference table where the two sets of lawyers argued, often employing terms she didn't understand, Pixie took Apollo's advice and acted accordingly and accidentally brought the table to a standstill of silence.

'You mean...' she finally grasped '... I get financially punished if I'm unfaithful but Apollo *doesn't*? How is that fair? I won't accept that.'

That was the instant when Apollo appreciated once

again that Pixie could take advice too literally and that characteristically she was seizing on something none of his father's wives had even picked up on. Not only had he underestimated her intelligence, he had also seemingly overlooked what appeared to be a very moral take on infidelity and his heart sank because he had never planned to be faithful during his marriage. He had planned to be very discreet but *not* faithful because only once in his life had he been faithful to a woman and it brought back appalling memories of betrayal and stupidity.

'Fidelity isn't a negotiable concept,' Pixie declared with even greater clarity.

And every man at the table studied Pixie as though she had landed on it wearing wings and carrying a flaming sword of justice.

'If Apollo is unfaithful he has to suffer for it,' Pixie completed with satisfaction, wondering why Apollo wasn't looking impressed that she had finally spoken up and behaved as a real bride-to-be surely would have done.

Apollo compressed his firm sensual mouth and studied the table. In point of fact billionaires who married penniless women didn't expect to suffer in *any* way when they finally got bored, least of all financially. Was this Pixie's clever way of trying to increase her divorce settlement? It had to be the money she was thinking about, the profit, he reasoned and then he glanced up and Pixie nailed him with grey eyes like volcanic rock and he realised that the issue of actual fidelity was one he had completely forgotten to discuss. Breathing in deep, he suggested a break for coffee.

Shown into an empty office, he studied Pixie. 'I wasn't planning to be faithful,' he admitted bluntly.

'Then this arrangement dies now. I'm not willing to

have sex with a man at the same time as he is having sex with other women!' Pixie declared in a wrathful undertone of ringing disgust.

'You're forgetting that this is a business arrangement.'

'Business arrangements don't normally include sex!' Pixie shot back at him defensively.

A faint line of colour accentuated Apollo's supermodel cheekbones. 'We have an *extraordinary* arrangement.'

'But you don't get to sleep with other women and me at the same time!' Pixie told him doggedly. 'That's immoral and I refuse to be part of it.'

It was what was called an impasse and Apollo had very rarely met with anything similar. Just when he was within an ace of making the first move towards his goal of regaining his birthright too! He gritted his teeth. 'I'll *try* to be faithful,' he framed in a roughened undertone of frustration.

But Pixie was seriously disappointed in Apollo. She hated cheats and had even less time for married men who played away. And Apollo might not love her and she might not love him but it was not unreasonable for her to expect him to treat her with respect.

'It's not going to look much like a real marriage if you're still acting like the biggest man whore in Europe!' Pixie flashed back at him, watching temper flare like burning flames in Apollo's green eyes and watching him bite it back. And why had he bitten it back? Because she had only stated the truth, she suspected.

And eventually they signed the pre-nuptial agreement with an addendum that stated that the bridegroom would 'endeavour' to remain faithful but relations were strained right round the table, both legal teams well aware that wedding fever was at a low ebb just at that moment. Apollo was merely relieved by the knowledge that he was flying out to Athens that evening. He was also reluctantly recalling that Vito had warned him that Pixie could be hot-headed and difficult and wondering if only his haste had persuaded him to overlook that distinct drawback. What else could it have been?

But how could she be so naïve and unreasonable as to demand fidelity from him? He knew what he was, hell, even *she* knew what he was! But he had promised to try and he would try because he stuck to his word, even if it choked him. And on some strange level he was conscious that her stance had made him respect her. She had standards and nothing he could offer would sway her from them.

CHAPTER FIVE

PIXIE TWIRLED IN front of the full-length mirror and smiled hesitantly because her glossy reflection was unfamiliar. Having enjoyed the attentions of a make-up artist and a grooming day at a salon recommended by Holly, Pixie had never before enjoyed such a level of sophisticated presentation.

'I really did think you'd choose to wear white,' Holly confided.

'White would be wasted on Apollo,' Pixie replied, wrinkling her nose and making Holly laugh. 'If I ever get to have a *real* wedding, I'll wear white.'

'I still can't believe you're marrying him. I was really shocked when Vito told me.'

Pixie sat down on the end of the bed and studied her linked hands. 'There's still stuff you don't know about the deal I made with Apollo,' she admitted uncomfortably because she could not bring herself to admit that sex and conception were involved, fearing that Holly would think badly of her for being so desperate that she would agree to a demand of that nature.

Yet while remaining fearful of the judgement of others, Pixie had made peace with that condition on her own behalf. She had always planned to become a mother some day, to have a child who was absolutely her own to love and nurture and protect. To fulfil that longing while married and to be assured of a future income with which to raise that child might yet prove to be the best chance she would ever get to have a baby and give it the happy childhood she had personally missed out on.

After all, she was no great shakes at dating, she acknowledged ruefully. She had always had to force herself out of the door to even socialise with men and the few she had taken the risk of spending time with had turned her off the notion entirely. Consequently she had decided that, left to her own devices, it was perfectly possible that she would've stayed single and alone and would never have had the opportunity to settle down with a partner and have a family. On that basis, she had decided that her agreement with Apollo Metraxis might well have advantages she had initially overlooked because, however briefly, she would get to experience being a wife and, hopefully, a mother.

Apollo had shared the test results that had come back on one of his calls from Athens. They were both healthy and normal as far as the entry-level testing they had had could establish. There was no obvious reason why they shouldn't conceive as a couple. He was still rather cool and clipped with her in tone because she had not seen him since they had parted at odds after that legal meeting, but Pixie had no regrets on that score. His fidelity while they were trying to conceive, as far as she was concerned, was non-negotiable. It wasn't much to ask, she reflected with faint bitterness and resentment; shouldn't it be a simple question of respect and decency? Apollo couldn't escape every moral obligation by throwing the 'business arrangement' label at her. But how hard would he 'endeavour' to meet her expectations? As a promise, it might well not be worth the paper it was written on.

'Well, you've finally told me about Patrick and there can't be anything worse than the mess he's got himself into, so I fully understand *why* you're doing this,' Holly said, squeezing her friend's shoulder soothingly. 'But you should've come to me for help.'

'Patrick's my problem, *not* yours,' Pixie pointed out with a hint of fierceness because her friend's desire to be generous with her money seriously embarrassed her. 'And this way I won't owe anyone anything. Apollo needs me as much as I need him and I prefer it like that.'

'It's a pity he's so...*so...*' Holly struggled to find a word, her cheeks colouring because it was occurring to her that now Pixie was marrying Apollo, even though it wouldn't be a proper marriage, possibly a little tact was required.

'He's been very good to Hector,' Pixie murmured thoughtfully. 'You know, rich or not, I don't think Apollo had it easy growing up either. Five stepmothers...what must that have been like for a little boy?'

'He's strong. He survived just like us. I suppose what I really wanted to ask is...how will you cope with his women?'

Pixie reddened and her pretty pearlised nails dug into the fabric of her wedding gown.

'Don't go falling for him, Pixie,' Holly warned her anxiously. 'He dumps women the instant they get clingy or needy and he seems to have the sexual attention span of a firefly.'

'Oh, I don't think I'm in any danger of making *that* particular mistake,' Pixie responded in a more relaxed tone of quiet confidence.

She lusted after Apollo and that was all and, as he himself had commented, that was a positive in their situation. The truth that he could make a single kiss that irresistible had been very persuasive. For the first time ever Pixie wasn't in fear at the prospect of having sex. Until he had opened his big mouth and referred to having sex in the limousine Apollo had made sex seem warm and intimate rather than sleazy, potentially painful and scary. He had also made it incredibly exciting.

Pixie's thoughts drifted much the way her dreams had throughout the week leading up to her wedding day, dreams filled with humiliating X-rated images that disturbed her sleep and woke her up hot and breathless and feeling quite unlike her usual sensible self.

Manfred arrived to tell them that the limo had arrived. Her foster mother, Sylvia Ware, was meeting them at the hotel where the civil ceremony would be staged because Holly had arranged transportation for the older woman. But Holly, Vito and Sylvia, as well as Pixie's brother and his partner, would be the only guests because it was to be a very small, quiet wedding, appropriate for a male who not only abhorred publicity but had also recently buried his father. Apollo had initially said no to her brother's attendance but had surprised her by giving way after she had argued that she had to somehow explain why she was leaving the UK. She had agreed not to tell Patrick the truth though.

Before she went into the private function room where the celebrant was staging the ceremony, Pixie paused to twitch her hair straight in a convenient mirror and breathed in very deep. On every level the step she was about to take daunted her because every aspect of living with Apollo Metraxis would be frighteningly new to her and Pixie only ever felt safe with what was familiar and harmless. Sadly, Apollo didn't fit into either category. But, true to her nature, Pixie lifted her head high, straightened her spine and her eyes glittered with deter-

mination as Holly opened the door for her to enter the
function room. Whatever she felt on the inside, however,
Pixie would conceal. Showing nerves and insecurities in
Apollo's radius would be like bleeding in the water near
a killer shark.

Apollo's rampant impatience lifted when the door opened.
She was five minutes late and for all of those five minutes he had wondered if she had got cold feet. Now with
the opening of that door his natural cynicism reasserted
its hold on him. Pixie was being very well rewarded for
marrying him and when had he ever known a woman
to turn her back on an opportunity to enrich herself? In
his experience, money talked much louder than anything
else. And then Pixie came into view.

And all such thoughts vanished at amazing speed from
Apollo's mind. She was wearing bright pink, not white,
and a short dress rather than a full-length one. And she
looked exactly like a tiny, very elaborate porcelain doll
in dainty heels. He stopped breathing, shimmering green
eyes locked to her delicate face beneath the feathery, dis-
tinctly un-bridal fascinator crowning her golden head.
For all her lack of height she looked ridiculously regal
with her hair swept up, her skin glowing, silvery eyes
wide and bright, bee-stung lips as pink as the gown. And
in only a few more minutes she would be *his* woman, he
reflected with a sudden deep satisfaction that was new
to him. *His* in a way no other woman ever had been or
would be in the future because there would be no more
marriages ahead of him. He had learned from his father's
mistakes that there was no perfect wife out there waiting if only you could find her, at least not if you were a
Metraxis and richer than sin. But still Apollo could not
look away from the vision his bride presented.

Pixie collided with emerald-green eyes that glittered like jewels below the thick black lashes longer than her own. Riveting. Powerful. *Hungry.* And she suffered a heady instant of disbelief that she could have that effect on Apollo, the notorious womaniser accustomed to females more beautiful than she could ever hope to be. She had tried so hard not to think of that aspect for comparisons of that nature were fruitless and would merely feed her anxieties in bed and out of bed with him. Colour ran riot up over her face because she had quite deliberately avoided reflecting on the end result of marrying Apollo... the wedding *night.* Would it be good or would her inexperience and his emotional detachment make it a disaster?

She reached his side and was dismayed to register that she was trembling. She had travelled in the space of seconds from telling herself that she was calm and composed to a jangling state of nerves that appalled her. As the celebrant began to read the wedding service, she forced herself to look up and encountered a searching look from Vito, who was smiling. Unnerved, she looked down again, her heart thumping very fast while Apollo threaded a ring onto her finger, his hand as warm and steady as hers was cold and shaky. *Lighten up, it's a business arrangement,* she reminded herself when the man and wife bit was pronounced and it was over and she believed she could relax again. At least she believed that for as long as it took Apollo to swing her round, his other arm sliding below her hips to lift her in what could only have been described as a caveman kiss.

He hauled her up to his level and his mouth crashed down on hers with passionate force. There was no warning, verbal or physical, simply that positively primeval public claiming that shocked Pixie anew. She had sensed the volatile nature pent up beneath the surface when Apollo had kissed her in his limousine but this kiss was a whole different experience. Before he had asked, this time he literally *took*, disdaining any preliminaries, both strong arms enclosed round her to keep her off the ground and raise her to his level. It took her breath away, it sent her heart thumping like a road drill, it stripped away every illusion that she had any form of control over him or herself. She could *taste* his sexual hunger and it speared through her like a heat-seeking missile, awakening every skin cell to raw new sensation.

It was wild and erotic and exciting but it was also ultimately terrifying for Pixie to feel unmanageable and wanton. For a frightening second, as he began lowering her back to the ground on legs that didn't feel they could possibly support her, she wanted to cling to his wide shoulders and stay exactly where she was. Instead she slid slowly down his big muscular body and not even his suit jacket could conceal the reality that he was as aroused as she was.

Shaken, she found her feet again, and Apollo closed a supportive arm round her lithe body. *His*, body and soul, whether she liked it or not. And he knew, he knew she wouldn't like it at all, and Apollo smiled with sudden blinding brilliance, raising a brow a little at his friend Vito's questioning appraisal and Holly's state of apparent incredulity. Pixie was his wife now and what happened between them was entirely his business and nothing to do with anyone else, he reflected with satisfaction.

Pixie glimpsed that smile and the colour already mantling her cheeks rocketed even higher, a pulse jumping at her collarbone because angry discomfiture was not far behind. With that kiss he had blown her cover story with Holly and she could see that even Vito was taken aback by Apollo's enthusiasm. In fact the only people not staring were Patrick, Maria and Sylvia, none of whom saw anything amiss with a passionate wedding kiss between the newly-weds. Pixie pulled away from Apollo to greet her foster mother, Sylvia, and thank her for her attendance, noting as she did that her brother was looking unusually stiff and troubled in comparison to his more usual carefree self.

Patrick kissed her cheek. 'What's wrong?' she whispered.

Holly tugged her away with an insistent hand on her arm. 'What haven't you told me?' she pressed in an undertone.

'Better you don't know,' Pixie whispered. 'Any idea what's up with my brother?'

'Vito said Apollo gave him a good talking to when he arrived,' her friend revealed. 'Not before time in my opinion. I think he frightened the life out of him about gambling.'

Fury shot through Pixie because she had always acted to the best of her ability as her brother's protector. It had hurt when they had ended up in separate foster homes, seeing each other only through occasional visits often set months apart. What did Apollo know about Patrick's life and what he had suffered? Or how proud Pixie was that her sibling had always had a job when so many other children who had been through the foster system ended up on the scrapheap of opportunity before they had even finished growing up? Yes, Patrick had got into trouble, and serious trouble at that, but that had happened two years ago and he had been paying for it ever since!

Apollo closed a big hand over hers and slotted a glass of wine into her other hand. 'We're eating now and then this nonsense will be over,' he framed with unhidden relief.

'What gave you the right to speak to my brother about his gambling?'

'He almost got you and himself killed the night you fell down those stairs,' Apollo countered with unblemished assurance. 'It was time someone showed him his boundaries.'

'That was not your right or your business,' Pixie hissed up at him like a stinging wasp, her anger unabated.

Apollo dealt her an unfathomable appraisal, his striking green eyes veiled. 'For as long as you remain my wife, everything that is your business will also be *mine*.'

'No, it isn't!' Pixie practically spat back at him in her ire.

'It's too late now to complain, *koukla mou*. That ring on your finger says very different,' Apollo spelt out without hesitation, and he swung round to stride back to Vito's side and laugh about something his friend was saying.

'Oh, dear,' Holly pronounced at her elbow. 'You're already fighting.'

Pixie was so enraged that she could hardly breathe and with difficulty she opened her mouth to say, 'Apparently, he regards a wedding ring on a woman's finger as something very like a slave collar.'

Holly giggled. 'That's only wishful thinking!'

And Pixie remembered her manners and asked after Holly's son, Angelo, who had remained in Italy with his nanny because his parents were only making a day trip to London. By the time that conversation concluded it was time to take their seats at the table and be served with the wedding breakfast. As time went on, Patrick's spirits picked up and he began to relax a little although his sister noticed he was visibly too scared to even look in Apollo's direction, never mind address him.

Sylvia insisted on making a very short speech, which

recounted a couple of tales about Holly and Pixie as teen-agers, which made everybody laugh. Vito wished them well, showing no sign of being tempted to make an attack on the bride as Apollo had done with his speech on his friend's wedding day.

'Watch yourself with Apollo's temper,' Holly whispered anxiously over the coffee. 'Vito says he can be very volatile.'

'Think I already know that,' Pixie muttered. 'As well as dictatorial, manipulative and sexist. I could go right through the alphabet with him and not one word would be kind, but then right now I'm angry.'

'When he saw you in that dress he stared at you as if you'd jumped naked out of a Christmas cracker. It was quite funny.'

Obviously, he hated the dress. Well, Pixie didn't care about that. She had gone shopping with her official personal stylist and had overridden her to make her own selections because, had Apollo's recommendations ruled, she would have ended up dressed like a middle-aged lady without fashion sense. Evidently, he didn't want her wearing normal *young* clothes, he wanted her tricked out in longer skirts and high necks. Well, he could just go jump off the nearest cliff with that wish, Pixie thought resentfully.

Why should he think he had the right to dictate the very clothes she wore? Wasn't she already surrendering enough with her freedom and her control over her own body? She was her own person and always had been and marrying Apollo Metraxis was not about to change that reality...

CHAPTER SIX

As Pixie prepared to clamber dizzily out of the helicopter, Apollo vaulted out and took her by surprise by swinging back and scooping her off her feet and carrying her off the helipad.

'I can walk!' Pixie snapped freezingly, feeling like an idiot as the yacht crew hanging around the helipad stared in apparent surprise at what was happening before their eyes.

'If I put you down you have to take your shoes off and walk barefoot. No heels on the decks,' Apollo delivered unapologetically.

'If I take my shoes off, I shrink into something pocket-sized!' Pixie hissed in a most un-bridal manner between gritted teeth.

Apollo shrugged a very broad shoulder. 'That's the rule. Blame your parents for your genes, not me.'

Pixie breathed in so deep to restrain her temper that she was slightly surprised she didn't spontaneously combust like a balloon overfilled with air. 'Put me down, Apollo.'

Holding her up with one arm as if to emphasise how strong he was, he flipped off her six-inch shoes with the other hand and carefully lowered her to the polished perfection of the deck surface. Pixie shrank alarmingly in stature and flexed angry bare toes on the sun-warmed wood. 'You're a dictator insisting on bare feet,' she condemned.

'Some things aren't up for negotiation,' he pointed out quite unnecessarily, striding past her to greet his yacht captain and shake hands, responding in a flood of his native Greek with a wide smile.

Feeling not remotely bridal, Pixie had a bouquet thrust in her arms and managed a beamingly polite smile while Apollo translated the captain's good wishes on what she privately termed their matrimonial nightmare.

What else could she call it when Apollo seemed to be racing off the rails in his resolve to do exactly as he liked regardless of how she might feel about it? She was still furious that he had confronted her brother about a matter she considered to be none of Apollo's business. Having that source of resentment followed by a very long flight in a helicopter that made her feel sick to board Apollo's giant yacht, *Circe*, in the Mediterranean had not improved her outlook. The ring on her wedding finger already felt very much like the slave collar she had mocked.

Long brown fingers guided her by her shoulder in the direction she was expected to go and she wanted to jump up and down and scream in frustration. Apollo was making her feel like a glove puppet. Go here, sit there, *do that*! It was as if he had swallowed the manual of *How to be a Control Freak with your Wife* at the same moment he was told he was married. She had seriously underestimated how very forceful and domineering he could be unless you did *exactly* as you were told. And there was no room for complaint, which he ignored.

'We need to clear the air about your brother,' Apollo announced, urging her into a room fitted out like an office with built-in cabinets, shelves and a very large desk.

'I will only tell you this one more time...' Pixie framed quite shakily but loudly in her rage. 'My brother is none of your business!'

Once again, Apollo ignored that statement. He extracted a slim file from a drawer in the desk and tossed it across the desk. 'Patrick is *still* gambling. Small card games with low stakes but he has a problem and it needs to be dealt with.'

'That's a complete lie and very unjust!' Pixie exclaimed.

'Pixie, there's sibling loyalty and then there's complete stupidity. Show me that you understand the difference and read the file.'

Her face flaming red with angry embarrassment, Pixie grabbed the file and retreated to a chair.

Apollo studied her with an air of exasperation. Why couldn't she understand that it was *his* job as a husband to protect her? That was all he was doing, as well as sorting out a problem that would only get worse if it was ignored. He had no personal axe to grind when it came to his brother-in-law. But it was obvious that Patrick was weak and in need of firm guidance. That had to be sorted out before Pixie's brother got himself into an even bigger mess because Apollo would refuse to settle the younger man's gambling losses if he got into trouble again.

Pixie's shoulders hunched as she read the investigation report, which stated that Patrick often played card games in the evening after he finished work. Her heart sank to her toes, the colour draining from her face to leave her stiff and pale. Her brother had lied to her and she was hugely hurt by that reality. He had *sworn* he would never gamble again, he had *sworn* he was not addicted but the evidence in the file proved otherwise and it was a total slap in the face for her to have to learn that fact from Apollo, who had all the sensitivity of a hammer blow.

'I had him investigated only as a precaution. I will not allow Patrick's difficulties to cause trouble between us. I tackled him today—in a *private* location, by the way—for your benefit and that of his partner,' Apollo informed her on a pious note that made his bride's teeth grit. 'Your brother has agreed to see an addiction counsellor and after her assessment he will follow the advice he receives. Otherwise his gambling debts will come back to haunt him—'

Pixie leapt upright in consternation. 'No, but you promised *me*!'

'The carrot and the stick approach *work*, Pixie,' Apollo cut in very drily. 'He needs a reason to reform and the child on the way is an excellent source of pressure on him to change his ways.'

'Holding that debt over him is so cruel, Apollo,' Pixie framed unevenly, grey eyes wide with stinging tears and accusation.

'He needs professional treatment and support. You are his sister, *not* his mother,' Apollo pronounced with finality. 'I won't change my mind about this, so don't waste your energy arguing about it.'

But Pixie already knew that she was unlikely to get anywhere arguing. Apollo was a steamroller, who travelled in a dead straight line and it was simply your bad luck if you lay in his path because he wouldn't deviate from his course.

Unhappily, his comment about her being Patrick's sister and not his mother lingered longest with Pixie, stirring up memories she would have sooner left buried. From an early age Pixie had been urged to look after her little brother. Her mother had *loved* Patrick in a way she had not seemed able to love her older child and that had stayed true right to the end of the older woman's life when she'd begged her daughter to always support her younger sibling.

As a child, Patrick had got treats, praise, affection and smiles from their mother while Pixie had been denied all of those things and left wondering what it was about her that made her less loveable. As she'd matured, however, she had come to suspect that her mother had been one of those women who would always have idolised her son in preference to her daughter, indeed who saw something almost magical in the mother-son bond from which she jealously excluded everyone else.

A knock on the door sounded and Apollo yanked it open and four little furry feet surged across the floor to boisterously attack Pixie's ankles. Damp-eyed, she bent down and lifted Hector, who was crazy happy to be reunited with her after a twenty-four-hour absence. He planted excited doggy kisses over her chin and made her reluctantly laugh as she petted him to calm him down.

'You need to get changed for dinner now,' Apollo informed her, gratified to have scored a coup by reintroducing the dog at the optimum moment. But then Apollo very rarely left anything to chance. He had planned that reunion as a soother almost as soon as he'd discovered that Patrick Robinson was still gambling because he had known that he had to confront his bride-to-be with the realities of the situation.

If you knew how to handle women, you could avoid conflict. Apollo had been smoothly and cleverly handling women since he was a child because his comfort had depended on the relationship he had established with his stepmothers. He avoided dramas with lovers in much the same style. An expensive piece of jewellery or a new wardrobe could work a miracle with an angry, resentful woman. Pixie, however, so far seemed infuriatingly indifferent to her new clothes and lifestyle but he had not yet had the chance to test her in that line. She could simply be faking her lack of interest, striving to impress him. He studied her tear-streaked face, the grey eyes soft now as she petted the tatty little dog she undoubtedly loved. He liked that she liked animals. It was the first time in a very long time that Apollo had actively *liked* anything about a woman and it shook him.

'You deliberately let me think that Hector and I were going to be apart for weeks,' Pixie condemned. 'Why did you do that? The carrot and the stick approach with me as well?'

Apollo shrugged. 'I dislike arguments. I knew you would be upset about your brother. Hector's your reward for accepting that I'm doing right by Patrick.'

Pixie's delicate frame went rigid. 'Stop trying to manipulate me, Apollo. If you want me to do something just face me with it. Try being honest for a change.'

Even barefoot she contrived to stalk out of the office to join the yacht steward waiting outside for her to show her to the master suite. On the trek there she was shown the gym, the medical centre, the sauna and steam room and the cinema. *Circe* was a massive vessel with four decks and seemed to contain everything Apollo might require to live on it on a permanent basis. He hadn't offered to give her a grand tour as she had somehow expected and now she scolded herself for imagining he might want to do something that normal. He didn't care what she thought of his yacht. He had to know that she had never been on a yacht before and was already utterly overwhelmed by the sheer opulence of her surroundings.

The huge stateroom with the massive bed, private deck and en-suite intimidated her but not as much as the stewardess who greeted her in perfect English as

'*Mrs* Metraxis' and asked her what she intended to wear. From the closets, Pixie picked out a black silky catsuit. So, she had to change for dinner now. Strange the traditions Apollo took for granted, she reflected helplessly as she tried not to let her gaze linger on the giant bed.

She was a bag of nerves but a couple of drinks would steady her, she told herself urgently. This was not the time to fall apart. Apollo wasn't going to hurt her. He wasn't going to attack her. In addition, he might be detached and she might only be a means to an end but he wasn't tactless enough to wrestle her out of her bra and then ask in a disappointed tone where her boobs had gone, as had once happened to Pixie. That experience, added to the guy who had told her that her lack of curves just didn't rev his engine, had been sufficient to kill Pixie's desire to get naked with a man simply to experiment. If truth be known she had envied Holly for the greater sexual confidence that had allowed her friend to sleep with Vito the first day she met him because Pixie knew that in the same circumstances she would have panicked and ended up saying no.

Only no wasn't quite an option with a wedding ring on her finger on their wedding night, particularly not with a male programmed to try and get her pregnant as fast as possible. She practised smiling in the mirror as she renewed her make-up and straightened her hair. She breathed in deep and strong as she dressed and tried not to fret at the trailing hems of the pant legs, which she had expected to wear with six-inch heels. The stewardess provided her with deck shoes and she thrust her feet moodily into them to be escorted to the dining saloon.

And there was Apollo awaiting her, resplendent in a tailored white dinner jacket and narrow black trousers that moulded long, powerful thighs, long black hair flaring round his lean, darkly handsome bronzed face. Gorgeous as a movie star and very, very sexy, she told herself bracingly, but complex as an algebraic equation to someone who had never got the hang of algebra.

She looked like a kid in the trailing pantsuit, Apollo reflected with hidden amusement. Why hadn't it occurred to her to wear something short? Her starlight eyes flickered with nervous tension over him and moved away hurriedly and he wondered why she was on edge because a woman expecting to share his bed had never been on edge with Apollo before. In fact most were enthusiastic, sparkling and downright impatient because he had a reputation for never sending a woman away dissatisfied.

He could see her nipples through the fine fabric because she wasn't wearing a bra and the tiny pouting shape of her breasts made him unexpectedly so hard that he ached, and he was forced to shift position to ease his discomfort while the wine was poured.

'How long will we be on the yacht for?' Pixie asked tautly.

Apollo shrugged, striking green eyes veiled. 'For as long as it takes us to get bored. I set up *Circe* to enable me to work wherever I am. We'll go to Nexos when we leave the yacht.'

'Nexos?'

'The Greek island my grandfather bought for the Metraxis family,' he extended. 'Of course, he had six children, of whom my father was the eldest, and the family was much bigger in his day. My father only had me. I have hundreds of cousins.'

'Didn't your father want any more children?'

'It wasn't an option. He eventually discovered that cancer treatment he had in his thirties had left him sterile. Had he had a check sooner, all his wives wouldn't have wasted their time pursuing fertility treatment,' Apollo admitted wryly. 'That's why I had the check.'

Pixie finished her first glass of wine and watched it being refilled by the silent waiter attending them. It unnerved her having a conversation with staff around but Apollo contrived to act as though they were alone.

The food was out of this world but Pixie felt that for all the enjoyment it was giving her she might as well have been eating sawdust. As the waiter left the saloon to fetch the dessert course, Apollo dealt her a frown. 'That's your fourth glass of wine.'

'You're counting?' she gasped in dismay.

'Should you be drinking at all with the project we have in mind?'

'I didn't think of that.' Pixie set her glass down. 'I don't know.'

'We have a doctor on board. I'll ask him. Aside of that aspect, I'm not having sex with you if you're drunk. That's something I would never ever do, regardless of whether or not we are married,' Apollo declared grimly.

Pixie reddened as if she had been slapped. 'I'm just a little nervous.'

Apollo stared at her with clear incomprehension. 'Why would you be?'

And Pixie knew that it was her moment to tell him the truth. After all, hadn't she urged him simply to be honest with her? Yet here she was covering up something very basic about her. But how could she tell a legendary womaniser that she was a virgin? He would think she was a freak or that no man had ever asked. It would be horribly humiliating. But worst of all, it would give Apollo a glimpse of her most intimate insecurities about herself and that was what Pixie couldn't bear. He would see her fear, her weakness, and he was ruthless and cold and he would use it against her, she thought wretchedly.

'Are you still hungry?' Apollo prompted softly.

'No,' she told him truthfully.

In a split second, Apollo rose from his chair and strode down to scoop her up out of hers, depriving her so thoroughly of breath and brain power that she merely stared up at him in astonishment. 'Time to make a start on that project, *koukla mou*,' he teased.

'You can put me down to walk.'

'I don't want you tripping and breaking a leg.'

'Of course...that would interfere with the project,' Pixie voiced for herself.

'I'm not that cold-blooded,' Apollo parried with a sudden husky laugh, glancing down at her with brilliantly striking green eyes. 'At this moment all I'm thinking about is that you're my wife and I *want* you.'

Pixie didn't believe that and an edge of panic infiltrated her. 'I'm not that experienced,' she told him abruptly.

Apollo smiled down at her, his wide sensual mouth tilting. 'How many guys?'

'A few,' she lied hastily, her face colouring, eyes veiling. 'I'm kind of fussy.'

Apollo liked being told that and rationalised that far from liberated thought with the reminder that she was his wife and naturally he didn't want a wife who had anything like his own track record. He knew that was sexist but it was the way he felt and it was a knee-jerk reaction that took him by surprise.

It was beginning to bother him that Pixie inspired such uncharacteristic urges. She was his wife but not a proper wife, he reasoned, merely the wife he had never thought he would have in the matrimonial step he had sworn never to take. And she was only with him in the first place because he had saved Patrick from the thugs her cowardly little brother had chosen to tangle with. It was a timely reminder but something visceral inside him denied that reminder because all of a sudden he discovered that he didn't like that either. He liked it much more when he looked down into Pixie's luminous grey eyes and read the same hunger that he was experiencing.

As he settled her down on the huge bed Pixie studied him, loving the strong angle of his jaw line, the starkness of his well-defined cheekbones and the classic jut of his nose, not to mention the lush black velvet sweep of his lashes shadowing those riveting emerald-green eyes. Looking at Apollo had the strangest intoxicating effect on her and her lips tingled as if in recollection of the kiss they had shared earlier.

He backed off a step and shed his jacket, embarked on his shirt and her heart started beating very, very fast inside her ribcage as he exposed the hard slab of his stomach and the incredibly defined muscles indenting his broad chest. He was drop-dead beautiful to her wide gaze. The shirt went flying. There was nothing inhibited about the speed with which he was stripping and she tried and failed to swallow as the trousers were unzipped and Apollo got down to boxers that revealed almost more than they concealed. He was already aroused, which shook and surprised her, indicating as it did that he did want her as he had declared he did.

But then, he clearly suffered from a high libido, she reminded herself, and possibly he was merely in the mood for sex and she was the only woman available. Yes, that made more sense to her. She would just be another nick on a bedpost already so full of nicks that hers would vanish into the woodwork. She tugged at the sleeves of her catsuit but he forestalled her, lifting her up in an in-furiatingly controlling way to turn her round and unzip the garment, sliding it off her stiff shoulders, tugging it down with all the smooth expertise of a male who could have stripped a woman out of the most intricate clothing in the dark without breaking a sweat.

Pixie trembled. He had even blocked her attempt to get a little tipsy. She was way more sober than she had planned to be, having assumed that the alcohol would make her less nervous. As it was she only felt the very slightest buzz from the wine she had imbibed before he made sobriety sound like her bounden duty.

Apollo was both disconcerted and enthralled by her sudden silence and submissive attitude for it was not at all what he had dimly expected from her. 'I'm not remotely kinky in bed if that's what you're worrying about,' he told her with amusement.

Pixie gulped. 'I'm not the slightest bit worried,' she assured him.

'Then why can't you relax and trust me?' Apollo en-quired lazily, his dark deep drawl having already dropped in pitch and the vowel sounds roughened.

In mortification, Pixie closed her eyes. 'I'd really pre-fer the lights out...'

'Not my preference but if that's what it takes, *koukla mou*.' Apollo reached up to stab a button above the head-board and the stateroom was plunged into darkness although soft light emanated from the lights still illumi-nating the private deck beyond the windows.

His wicked mouth descended on the slope of her neck and she shivered, a different kind of tension entering her now that he no longer had an alarmingly bright view of her physical deficiencies. She quivered as long fingers expertly teased her straining nipples.

'I'm very small there,' she pointed out, unable to resist a ridiculous urge to draw his attention to the obvious.

'I like it,' Apollo growled next to her ear, nipping at her ear lobe, sending another shot of uncontrolled response darting through her.

'Men always want more, not less.'

Apollo arched his hips and ground his pelvis against her thigh. 'Does that feel like I'm low on sexual interest?' he asked silkily. 'Now, be quiet.'

And Pixie shut her mouth because she was embarrassed by the inappropriate comments spilling from her lips. He rested her against the soft pillows and employed his mouth on her breasts, sending increasingly powerful streams of sensation down into her pelvis. Her hips rocked of their own volition and that shocked her. She could feel herself getting hot and damp there and that shocked her almost as much as her sudden desire to join in and explore him. Of course, she didn't have the nerve. She lay there like a felled statue, settling for being hugely grateful not to be on the edge of a panic attack.

Apollo was wheeling out his entire repertory of foreplay in an attempt to win the fireworks response he had craved from their first kiss. He had never gone so slowly in his life with a woman. He had never had to because usually they were all over him, egging him on to the final act as if afraid he would lose interest if it took too long to get there. He kissed a line down a slender arm and smiled. There was just nothing of her and he would have to be very careful not to crush her. He caressed a tiny foot, flexed the toes, revelling in the novelty of that fragile daintiness. She might be small but everything was in perfect proportion. As he skimmed down her panties he reached up, fingers closing into her golden hair to raise her head and claim her lips again.

A gasp was wrenched from Pixie as he nuzzled her lips with his, brushed them gently apart and then went in for the kill with his tongue and it was as if the top of her head blew off. When Apollo kissed her she literally saw stars and heavenly galaxies. With every caressing, darting plunge of his tongue her temperature rocketed and her still hands finally rose and plunged into the depths of his hair. Finally getting that response energised Apollo's hunger.

There was so much he wanted to do that he didn't know where to begin but he knew he wanted it to be an unforgettable night for her. Why it had to be that way with her he didn't know or care, but then he had always responded very well to a challenge and in many ways Pixie had challenged him right from the start. Unimpressed, cool, indifferent. For the first time in his life Apollo wanted a needy, clingy woman and he didn't understand the desire or where it was coming from.

He spread her legs and shifted down the bed. Pixie froze as if he'd suddenly put the lights back on. He wanted to do *that*?

'I don't think I want that,' she told him hastily.

'You'll be surprised,' Apollo husked, ready to rise to yet another challenge and embarking on the venture with a long daring lick that made her squirm and gasp again. Satisfied, he settled in to drive her crazy. He would be the very best she had ever had in bed or he would die trying. Lack of interest would become craving. Coolness would become heat. Unimpressed would become awed.

Apollo touched her with expert delicacy that she knew she couldn't object to although she couldn't imagine that he could possibly *want* to do what he was doing. He slid a finger into her damp folds and she almost spontaneously combusted in shock and excitement and that was nothing compared to the intense feel of his mouth on the tiny bundle of nerves at the apex of her. All of a sudden control was something she couldn't reclaim because her body had a will of its own. Her hips ground into the mattress below her, her heartbeat thundered and she was breathing so loud she could hear it while the growing tightness deep down inside her was impossible to ignore. She could feel herself, reaching, straining, while the ripples of excitement grew closer and closer together and then an almost terrifying wave of ecstasy gripped her and she was flying and crying out and moaning all at the same time.

'When you come the next time, I want you to say my name,' Apollo growled in her ear while her body still trembled in shock from the sheer immensity of what he had made her experience.

'Never felt like that before,' Pixie mumbled unevenly.

'It will *always* feel like that with me,' Apollo assured her with great satisfaction as he slid over her, tilting her hips up to receive him, and drove down into her with an uninhibited groan of all-male need.

Pixie jerked back in shock from the sharp pain that assailed her and yelped in dismay.

But Apollo had already stopped. He raised himself higher on his arms to instantly withdraw from her again and folded back at her feet, the sheet tangled round him. His lean, darkly handsome face was a mask of disbelief. 'You're kidding me?'

Pixie sat up with a wince because she was sore and way more conscious of that private part of her than she wanted to be. She was still in too much shock to think because she had long dismissed as an old wives' tale the concept of a first sexual experience hurting and had been entirely unprepared to discover otherwise.

'A...*virgin*?' Apollo gritted in much the same tone of

disdain as he might have mentioned a rat on board his superyacht.

Anger began to lace her growing mortification. 'Why did you have to stop?' she gasped, stricken. 'Couldn't you just have got it over with?'

'Like you know so much about it?' Apollo virtually snarled at her as he vaulted off the bed with the air of a man who couldn't get away quickly enough from the scene of a disaster. A little warning voice at the back of Apollo's volatile head was warning him to tone it down but he was genuinely furious with Pixie for wrecking something with her silence that he had been determined to make special. Special...*really*? Where had that goal come from inside him? *Why?* He didn't know but he was still furious about the bombshell she had dealt him when he'd least expected it.

'Maybe I should have warned you,' Pixie framed tightly, recognising that he was sincerely annoyed with her.

'There's no maybe about it!' Apollo thundered back at her. 'I *hurt* you and how do you think that makes me feel? I gave you every opportunity to tell me and you didn't.'

'I thought you'd laugh at me.'

Apollo shot her a narrowed green glance. 'Do I look like I'm laughing?'

Pixie swallowed hard, her face burning at his raw derision. Clutching the sheet to her bare skin, she felt about an inch high while she watched him striding into the bathroom, over six feet of lean golden-skinned enraged male.

What did *he* have to be so annoyed about? She hadn't thought of her body as his business until they got into bed but then suddenly, she registered, it *had* become his business. Discomfiture gripped her. He was accustomed to experienced women and probably feeling out of his depth after she'd yelped cravenly at one small jab of pain. Really, could she possibly have made more of a fuss? Was it any wonder that he was angry?

Guilt stirring, Pixie slid out of bed and pulled on his shirt, because it was the nearest item of clothing that would cover her. She breathed in the scent of him almost unconsciously and sighed because she had screwed up, made a mountain out of what would probably have been a molehill had she simply been a little more frank in advance. But being frank on such a personal topic was something Pixie had never contrived to be, even with Holly.

As she appeared in the doorway Apollo glowered at her from the shower, standing there naked and unconcerned, water streaming from several jets down the length of his big bronzed body. Pixie stared and flushed. 'I'm sorry,' she said grudgingly. 'I should've warned you.'

'But instead of warning me, you actually *lied*!' Apollo condemned emphatically, still struggling to work out why he was so angry when he very rarely got angry about anything. A virgin—very unexpected but scarcely a hanging offence. That she had lied to him annoyed him more because, most ironically, she was the first woman he had ever believed to be more honest than was good for her.

'I said sorry. There's not much more I can do,' Pixie launched back at him a little louder, her temper rising. 'What do you want? Blood?'

'Already had that experience with you,' Apollo derided smooth as polished glass.

And that crack was the last straw for Pixie and she lost it. Her fingernails bit into her palms as her hands fisted and she shot a look of loathing at him that startled him. 'You're just reminding me why I don't like men and *why* I didn't warn you,' she framed jerkily, formerly suppressed emotion surging up through her slight body in a great heady surge.

'And why would that be?' Apollo demanded, switching off the water, grabbing up a towel and stalking out of the shower.

'Because you're threatening and selfish and mean! I put up with far too much of that growing up!' she told him in a screaming surge. '*Men* trying to catch me with my clothes off when I was in the bathroom or the bedroom...*men* trying to touch me places they shouldn't... *men* saying dirty stuff to me...'

Apollo had seemingly frozen where he stood. Not even the towel he had been using to dry himself was moving. 'What men?'

'Care staff in some of the children's homes I stayed in, foster fathers...sometimes the older boys in the homes,' she related shakily, caught up in the frightening memories of what she had endured over the years before she'd reached Sylvia's safe house and then eventually moved towards complete independence. 'So, don't be surprised I was still a virgin! Sex always seemed sleazy to me and I'm not apologising for it. Not everyone's obsessed with sex like you are!'

Listening, Apollo had lost all his natural colour and much of his cavalier attitude. His bone structure was very stark beneath his golden tan. 'You were abused,' he almost whispered the words.

'Not in the strictest sense of the word,' Pixie argued defensively. 'I learned to keep myself safe. I learned that what they were doing was wrong. Nobody ever actually managed to *do* anything but it put me off the physical stuff...'

'Obviously...naturally.' Apollo snatched in an almost ragged breath and veiled green eyes rested on her. 'Go

back to bed and try to get some sleep. I won't be disturbing you.'

Taken aback, Pixie stared without comprehension at
his tight, shuttered expression.

'I'm sorry I hurt you.'

'It was only a tiny hurt. I just wasn't expecting it,' she
muttered awkwardly, but she could see that even that little
hurt and the surprise of it had been a complete passion
killer as far as he was concerned.

Apollo strode back into the bedroom and she heard
him rummaging through the drawers in the dressing
room. Moments later he stepped back into view sheathed
in tight faded denim jeans and a white linen shirt and,
without even pausing to button the shirt, he strode out
of the stateroom. So much for their wedding night, Pixie
thought wretchedly. Getting into bed he had definitely
wanted her, lusted after her, and what had preceded the
final act had been fantastic. He had given her an ecstasy
she had not known she was capable of feeling. But all
too quickly she had blown it…

CHAPTER SEVEN

WHAT WERE THE ODDS? Apollo asked himself as he sat on deck swigging from a bottle of Russian vodka, his black hair blowing back from his lean darkly attractive features, his green eyes very bright. What were the odds that he would end up with a woman who had also been abused? Whose attitude to sex had been inexorably twisted and spoiled by experiences that had happened when she was too young to handle them?

Not only had he hurt her physically, he had also *shouted* at her. Half a bottle further on, Apollo padded barefoot over to the rail. His wife was a virgin and he had acted like an idiot. Why? He was an arrogant jerk proud of his sexual skill and finesse…why not just admit that? He had been so determined to give her the fantasy and it had gone pear-shaped because she hadn't trusted him enough to tell him the truth. And how could he hold that against her when throughout his whole thirty years of life he had never told anyone but his father what had happened to him? He knew about that kind of secret; he *knew* about the shame and the self-doubt and the whole blame game. And even though he had seen slivers of low self-esteem and insecurity and anxiety in Pixie it had not once occurred to him that she too could be something of a victim, just like him.

She had deserved better, much better than he had given her. He had treated her like one of the good-time girls he normally enjoyed, confident and experienced women who wanted fun and thrills in and out of bed and as much luxury and cash as they could wheedle out of him. That had suited him because it left him in complete control at all times. But he wasn't in control with Pixie and that seriously disturbed him. He was clever, he was normally cool and logical and yet instead of being delighted that his wife had never been with another man he had shouted at her.

And paradoxically he *was* delighted because something about Pixie brought out a possessive vibe in him and that vibe of possessiveness had lit up and burned like a naked flame the instant he'd married her. Furthermore, since she had had the courage to tell him something as personal as what she had spilled out in her distress in the bathroom, he really did owe her, didn't he?

Apollo wove his path rather drunkenly back to his stateroom where he tripped over the clothes Pixie had gathered up and left in a heap directly in line with the door. The racket he made hitting the floor and his yell of surprise yanked her out of her miserable thoughts with a vengeance.

Fumbling for the bedside light, Pixie switched it on and stared in wonderment at Apollo sprawled in a heap on the floor. 'What happened to you?'

'I got drunk, 'Apollo informed her with very deliberate diction.

'After a…a crummy night that makes sense.'

'Don't be all English and polite and nice,' Apollo groaned, raking a hand through his tousled black hair. 'I wasn't.'

'But then you're not English,' Pixie parried, marvelling at the vision of her very controlled new husband in such a condition. His green eyes had a reckless glitter that unnerved her a little. Sober, he was a lot to handle. Drunk, he could well be more than she could manage.

'Never been with a virgin before,' he confided. 'I wanted it to be perfect and then it went wrong and I was furious. My ego, my pride, nothing to do with you. I was a…' He uttered a four-letter swear word.

'Pretty much,' she agreed more cheerfully after hearing that he had wanted their wedding night to be perfect, which was a hearteningly unexpected admission when deep down in advance of the bed business she had feared that he would not care a jot. She relaxed her stiff shoulders into the pillows while she studied him and decided that even drunk he was heartbreakingly gorgeous.

'My second stepmother beat me with a belt and left me covered with blood,' Apollo announced out of the blue.

Her jaw dropped. 'How old were you?'

'Six. I hated her.'

'I'm not surprised. What did your dad do?'

'He divorced her because of it. He was very shocked… but then he was sort of naïve about how cruel women can be,' Apollo told her as he drank out of the bottle still clutched in one big bronzed hand, lean muscles rippling to draw her attention to the intricate dragon tattoo adorning his arm. 'He didn't appreciate that *I* was the biggest problem in his remarriages.'

'How?' Pixie asked, wondering if she should try to get the bottle off him or just close her eyes to it. He wasn't acting like himself. He might hate her tomorrow for having seen him in such a vulnerable mood.

'When a woman marries a very rich man *she* wants to be the one who produces his son and heir but I was already there and the apple of my father's eye.'

'By the sound of that beating you got, he wasn't look-ing after his apple very well.'

Apollo closed his eyes, black lashes almost hitting his cheekbones. 'He married my third stepmother when I was eleven. She was a very beautiful Scandinavian and the only one who seemed to take a genuine inter-est in me. Never having had a mother, I was probably starved of affection.' His shapely mouth quirked. 'She would come and visit me at school and stuff. My father was very pleased and encouraged her every step of the way.'

'So?' Pixie prodded, sensing the tripwire coming in the savage tension bracketing his beautiful mouth, the warning that all could not have been as cosy as he was making it sound.

'Basically she was grooming me for sex. She liked adolescent boys...'

'You were eleven!' Pixie condemned. 'Surely you weren't capable.'

'By the time she took me to bed I was thirteen. It went on for two years. She took me out of school to city ho-tels. It was sordid and deviant and I was betraying my own father but...*but* she was my first love and I was fool enough to worship the ground she walked on. I was her *pet*,' he completed in disgust.

Pixie leapt out of bed and darted across the floor to kneel down in front of him. 'You were...what age?'

'Fifteen when I got caught with her.'

'For two years a perverted woman preyed on you.'

'I wasn't even her only one,' Apollo bit out in a slur-ring undertone. 'She'd been meeting up with the son of a local fisherman on the beach. It was *his* father who went to mine and tipped him off about what she was like.'

Pixie shifted until she was behind him and wrapped

her arms round his rigid shoulders. 'You were just a kid. You didn't know any better.'

'I definitely knew it was wrong to have sex with my father's wife,' Apollo broke in curtly. 'I don't deserve forgiveness for that but he still forgave me.'

'Because he loved you,' Pixie reasoned. 'And he knew his wife was using you for her own warped reasons. I'm so sorry I called you a man whore. You had a really screwed-up adolescence and of course it affected you.'

Apollo reached behind himself to yank her round and tumble her down into his lap. 'I never told anyone about that before…until you told me tonight about growing up in care with men trying to hit on you or spy on you or whatever,' he mumbled into her hair, the words slurring. 'Now I think I need to go to bed before I fall asleep on top of you, *koukla mou*.'

Pixie got up and removed the bottle while he stripped where he stood and, only staggering very slightly, fell like a tree into the bed. He slept almost immediately and she watched him in the half-light for long minutes, thinking how wrong she had been about him once and how much better she now knew him. Yet with what he had revealed he seemed more maddeningly complex than ever and without a doubt the man she had married in a business arrangement absolutely fascinated her. She brushed his tumbled black hair back from his brow and slid into the other side of the bed, hesitating only a moment before edging closer to take advantage of Apollo, whose natural temperature seemed to be the equivalent of a furnace.

She surfaced to dawn very, very slowly, the insistence of her body awakening her to a sweet flood of sensations. It was still so novel for her to feel such things that she knew instantly it was Apollo touching her and just as quickly she relaxed. Her nipples had tightened into needy little buds and the delicate place where his clever fingers were playing was embarrassingly sensitive and wet.

'You awake now?' he prompted gruffly in her ear.

'Yeah...' she framed weakly, her hips moving all on their own because the magical way he touched her made her ache, need and want all over again.

Apollo shifted over her, all rippling muscle and ferocious control. Green eyes glittered down at her, his lean, strong face taut and dark with stubble. She felt him at the heart of her and anxiety screamed that there was too much of him for what little there was of her so it was a struggle to force herself not to stiffen. Fortunately, he went slow—achingly slow—and she gradually stretched around his fullness, tender tissue reacting with unexpected pleasure to the source of that amazing friction. He shifted his hips, moved and a rush of exhilarating feelings engulfed her and her head fell back, eyes wide with surprise.

'Didn't want to give you the chance to get all nervous again,' Apollo admitted. 'Like it was likely to be some sort of punishment.'

'Definitely...*not*...punishment,' she gasped breathlessly, her body rising to meet the gathering power of his, excitement pooling like liquid fire in her pelvis.

'Just sex,' he told her.

And had she still had breath to disagree she would have done but she couldn't breathe against the rising tide of intoxicating excitement. Little undulating tingles of intense arousal were travelling in tightening bands through her trembling length. He was inside her and over her and nothing had ever felt that good or that powerful. Apollo smiled down at her, a smile ablaze with male satisfaction and, for once, she didn't mind his assurance. He gathered up her legs and angled her back, rising higher, thrusting faster, deeper, forcing little moans and cries from her parted lips that she couldn't hold back. The excitement intensified, sensation tumbling on sensation until a sensual explosion detonated deep within her and she went flying high and free on an electrifying surge of pleasure.

Apollo groaned his appreciation into her hair and she wrapped her arms round him. It was automatic, instinctive, something of a shock when he broke immediately free and imposed space between them. His lean, darkly handsome face had shuttered. 'I can't do that stuff,' he muttered semi-apologetically, his beautifully shaped mouth momentarily rigid with tension.

And Pixie forced a smile she didn't feel and shifted back in turn because she got it, she really did get it after what he had explained the night before. A child crying out for maternal affection, initially given it only to discover that it was an evil deception being utilised to gain his trust and love.

She swallowed the thickness in her throat and fought a very strong urge to hug him. He was the only man who had ever had that much power over her and momentarily it scared her. Sometimes Apollo made her want to kick him very hard and then equally suddenly she wanted to put her arms round him instead, even though she knew he didn't want that, couldn't handle that… It wasn't only her body he could make fly out of control: somehow he was reaching her emotions as well, and she knew that was dangerous and she tensed.

Apollo was intensely uncomfortable for a male accustomed to feeling at home in virtually every situation. He very rarely drank to excess and when he did he could still control his tongue, yet inexplicably he had lost control the night before and confided his deepest secrets. He understood that her experiences had reanimated memories he had suppressed and that that had destabilised him but that didn't mean he had to like his own weakness. He really didn't like that sudden feeling of being exposed and vulnerable because it reminded him too much of his lost childhood. For that reason it felt good to have a distraction available.

'I've got something for you,' he told her, reaching into the drawer by the bed to produce the jewellery case he had stashed there several days before. Apollo always thought out everything well in advance, preparing for every eventuality if he could. And she *deserved* a gift much more than the women who usually shared his bed.

The wedding night, after all, had been pretty much disastrous and his getting drunk and telling all in such a girly fashion, Apollo reflected grimly, had crowned the disaster. She had tolerated it all and in spite of everything that had gone wrong she had still lain back trustingly for him to claim her body even though she had feared that consummation.

Taken aback, Pixie stared down in astonishment at the case and then carefully opened it. A breathtaking bracelet ran in a river of glittering diamonds across the velvet inset. 'For me?'

'Wedding present,' Apollo pronounced with relief as he leapt out of bed with alacrity and headed for the shower, convinced that he had done the very best that he could to be thoughtful and decent.

'It's gorgeous and I suppose I need some jewellery to make me look like a proper rich wife,' Pixie murmured uncertainly, battling to rise above hurt feelings she knew she had no right to experience. 'But this was a bad time to give it to me.'

Apollo's long lashes fanned down in disbelief and

he gritted his white teeth before he swung back to her. 'How so?'

Pixie contemplated him as he stood there, buck naked, bronzed and very Greek godlike in his physique. He was without a doubt the most physically beautiful male she would ever be with but, time and time again, he confounded her and wounded her. 'I'm not some whore you have to pay for a one-night stand.'

'I've never been with a professional,' Apollo said icily. 'I gave you a gift. Thanks would have been the appropriate response.'

'It's just the way *this* makes me feel,' Pixie began, struggling to verbalise what she didn't quite understand herself.

'We have a business arrangement,' Apollo shot back at her unapologetically. 'Think of it as business.'

'I can't think of my body as business. I'm not sure what that would make me,' Pixie admitted unhappily. 'But I need more respect than you're giving me if we're going to be stuck together like this for months. I don't think that's too much to ask. Obviously you can't even bring yourself to put your arms round me after sex. I'm not going to turn clingy or needy, Apollo. I'm not about to fall in love with you or the things you can buy me either. I know this marriage isn't real.'

A whine sounded from below the bed.

'Shush, dog,' Apollo groaned in raw frustration. 'You've been walked, you've been fed and watered. Stay out of this…she's enough to handle without your input.'

Pixie had to bite her tongue not to comment on the reality that she had overlooked her beloved pet's needs and Apollo had not. Instead she forced herself to continue. 'Couldn't we try friendship if we can't have anything else that might make you feel threatened?'

Apollo flung back his arrogant dark head and green eyes radiated emerald fire in the sunlight. 'You do *not* make me feel threatened.'

Pixie surrendered and said exactly what was on her mind. 'Don't punish me because you talked too much for your own comfort last night.'

And there it was in a nutshell, what Apollo Metraxis absolutely couldn't *stand* about Pixie. Somehow, *Thee mou*, she saw beyond the surface and saw right *through* him and it was the most unnerving experience he had had in many years. Without another word, Apollo strode into the shower, hit every dial, turned up the pressure and refused to think by blanking out everything, a trick he had learned as a child to stay in control. He held himself straight and taut until the confusion and bewilderment and seething frustration drained fully away with the swirling water.

Suppressing a groan of equal frustration, Pixie tunnelled back down into the bed and made no objection when Hector jumped up to tuck himself in next to her body. Hopefully Apollo would think she was sleeping in. Instead of sleeping, however, she was counting pluses, a habit she had formed as a child to make a grey day look sunnier. Number one, she enumerated, they had done the sex thing and it had been...amazing. Number two, Apollo was damaged but at least he had explained why, even if he did regret it. Number three, he was *trying* to make the marriage work but he hadn't a clue how to meet such a challenge. Female partners who whooped over his financial generosity and who only lasted for a two-week session of nightly sex didn't provide a man with much of an education on how to make a woman feel happy, respected and secure. Was she expecting too much from him? This was supposed to be a business arrangement, she reminded herself ruefully. Maybe *she* was being unreasonable...

Pixie breakfasted alone on the polished deck with Hector at her feet: Apollo was working. He had *phoned* her to make that announcement in a very detached voice that suggested he suspected he could be dealing with a potential screaming shrew. As far as avoidance techniques went, Apollo had nothing whatsoever to learn. When her phone went off again she answered it unhurriedly, assuming there was something he wished to tell her, but this time it wasn't Apollo, it was Holly.

'Vito and I are flying out to join you this afternoon!' Holly exclaimed excitedly. 'What do you think?'

Pixie rolled her eyes. 'The more the merrier,' she quipped, oddly hurt that Apollo had to bring in other people to create yet another barrier between them within a day of the wedding. Was she really that unbearable? She flexed her fingers against her flat stomach and prayed to get pregnant *fast*. The sooner she and Apollo escaped the situation they were in and separated, the better it would be. If they weren't living together and sharing a bed, it would be easier to stick to a businesslike attitude, she reasoned, wondering why her heart now felt as heavy as lead.

'We're all heading to some nightclub on Corfu tonight,' Holly told her. 'Of course, you'll already know that...sorry, I'm talking a mile a minute here.'

Quite unaware that yet another attempt to please Pixie had bombed dismally, Apollo stayed in his office on board until he got word that their guests were arriving.

'I promise not to ask any awkward questions,' Holly whispered as she settled on the end of the bed in Apollo and Pixie's stateroom. 'But you don't look happy and I can't imagine we'd be getting hauled in last minute if you were. Am I allowed to ask about that?'

Pixie grimaced. 'No. I'm sorry.'

'No need to be sorry but you sound attached…and the weird thing is Apollo is sounding attached too—'

'No, that's definitely not happening,' Pixie cut in with confidence.

'Apollo told Vito he wanted us here because he thought it would please you. Vito's never known him to make that much effort for a woman.'

Unimpressed, Pixie shrugged and watched Holly pet Hector while Angelo explored the room in the vain hope of finding something to play with. Bending down, she scooped her godson up intending to get reacquainted with the adorable toddler.

'So, what are you wearing tonight?' Holly prompted, taking the hint.

Relieved by the change of subject, Pixie showed off her outfit.

'My goodness, I'll look so old-fashioned next to you. What time are you getting your hair done?'

'I'm doing my own hair,' Pixie countered in surprise.

'You've got a beauty salon on board and you're *still* going to do it yourself?'

As soon as Holly had realised that Pixie hadn't even known the *Circe* had a full-time grooming parlour for guests and had commented bluntly on Apollo's deficiencies as a husband and a host, the two women set off on an exploration tour designed to satisfy both and entertain Angelo.

Hours later, after a convivial dinner during which Apollo contrived to ignore the reality that he had a wife seated at the same table, which resulted in Pixie going to even more extreme lengths to ignore him, Pixie emerged on the lower deck, fully dressed and ready to board the motor boat waiting to whisk them out to the island of Corfu.

Apollo studied his wife in consternation, his lean dark face taut and cool. 'I don't like the clothing,' he said baldly.

Vito actually flinched and walked Holly over to the deck rail several yards away.

Pixie jerked a narrow bare shoulder in dismissal of the comment. She wore a skintight cerise-pink leather corset and a fitted black pencil skirt with very high heels. It was young and hip and she didn't much care what he thought about it. 'You can command everything else, Apollo, but *not* what I wear. What's your objection anyway?'

His strong jaw line squared. 'You're showing too much of your body.'

'I've heard you've been seen with women who don't even bother with underwear.'

'You're different…you're my wife,' Apollo declared grimly. 'I don't want other men looking at my wife.'

'Tough,' Pixie commented with a combative glint in her grey eyes. 'You're a Neanderthal in a suit.'

'If we didn't have guests, I wouldn't allow you off the boat!' he growled half under his breath.

What a complete hypocrite he was! Pixie thought in wonderment, helpless amusement lacing her defiance. Apollo was a living legend for entertaining women who looked as though they had left half their outfit at home to maximise the exposure of their perfect bodies.

A couple of hours later, amusement had become the last thing on Pixie's mind. She was huddled in the luxury

VIP cloakroom of the club with Holly. 'I'm sorry you've been dragged into this,' she muttered apologetically.

'What? Watching Apollo behave badly? I shouldn't say it but it's his favourite pastime.'

Pixie tossed her head, golden blonde hair dancing round her shoulders, her piquant little face vivid with anger and mortification. 'I can behave badly too...'

Holly pulled a face. 'But provocation is not the road I would take with Apollo.'

Pixie, however, was past being polite and low-key and sensible. Since their arrival at the nightclub Apollo had been swamped by women. He was extremely well-known on the club circuit and he had not made a single attempt to deter the rapacious females trying to pick him up. Pixie had watched in wooden silence while other women pitched themselves onto her husband's lap, danced in front of him in very suggestive ways and squeezed up close to him. He had bought them drinks and chatted to them as if Pixie were the invisible woman and she had had enough of his treatment. She had also learned why he made no effort with her. From what she could see by the over-eager girls surrounding him, Apollo had never *had* to make an effort. He was very hot and very rich and acting like a kid let loose in a candy shop was the norm for him.

Pixie took her cocktail over to the VIP rail and watched the dancers because she loved to dance. Much good it was doing her though, she reflected moodily, wincing at the high-pitched giggling travelling from their crowded table. She wanted to empty entire ice buckets over Apollo and then kick him from one end of *Circe* to the other. Friends, she had suggested mildly, and *this* was the answer he was giving her? And why did she care? Why on earth did she care? She glanced at him out of the corner of her eye and watched a woman run her fingers down his broad chest and her teeth clenched with something that felt very like rage.

'Would you like to dance?' a faintly accented and unfamiliar voice said from behind her.

Pixie spun round and found herself virtually eye to eye with a black-haired good-looking young man with very dark eyes and an Eastern cast of feature and she smiled. Vito had asked her to dance and she had said no, recognising pity when she saw it, and she had said no to Holly too, but a total stranger was a perfectly acceptable substitute for a husband who was ignoring her while simultaneously outraging her sense of decency.

'Yes, thank you...' Pixie acquiesced, noticing how all four of the bodyguards who had accompanied their party from the yacht all rose as one at a nearby table. With determination she smiled to let them know that she was pleased to have company and not in need of rescue.

'I am Saeed,' her companion informed her.

'I'm Pixie,' she said cheerfully, preceding him down the stairs, noting that two of Apollo's bodyguards were now taking up position at the edge of the dance floor alongside two large men of a similar look.

'Where's Pixie?' Apollo asked Holly abruptly.

'Dancing,' Holly announced somewhat smugly.

'With another man?' Apollo demanded with savage incredulity and he flew upright.

Vito sprang up as well and accompanied his friend to the rail that overlooked the floor below. 'You can't thump him. He holds diplomatic status and he's half your size. It would make you look bad.'

At his elbow, Apollo swore wrathfully in four different languages as he finally picked out his wife and her partner from the crowd. He watched Pixie wriggle her diminutive behind while her partner gripped her hips and drew her close. Blinding rage filled him as the other man bent his wife back in a dip that brought their bodies into intimate contact and he strode down the stairs with Vito flying to keep pace with him.

'He's an Arab prince...don't hit him and cause a scene!' Vito warned.

Apollo's powerful hands coiled into fists of fury. What the hell did Pixie think she was playing at? She was his wife and she wasn't allowed to let *any* other man touch her body! He never ever lost his temper, he reminded himself fiercely, but there she was, twitching every inch of that lithe, dainty little body and the Arab Prince wasn't the only one noticing that tight skirt and that fitted little top that showed the slope of her gorgeous breasts. In an almighty storm of rage Apollo acted in what for him was a very diplomatic manner. He stepped up behind Pixie and hauled her off her feet and threw her over his shoulder.

'She's my wife!' he grated down at the startled Prince, who was the same size as Pixie in her heels, which wasn't very tall, and with that clear announcement of his God-given right to interfere Apollo strode off for the exit.

It took several annoying seconds for Pixie to realise what was happening but she instantly recognised Apollo's scent. She pounded his back with clenched fists and screamed at him full volume, 'What the hell do you think you're doing? Put me down right this minute!'

His bodyguards studiously not looking near either of them, Apollo stuffed his wife in the limo that would take them back to the harbour. Like a spitting cat, Pixie launched herself at him to try and get back out of the car again. 'I want to go back and join Vito and Holly!' she yelled.

Apollo drew in a deep shuddering breath and said as mildly as he could, 'You're going back to the yacht and if that's how you intend to behave when I take you out it'll be a long time before you get out again.'

'You can forget that option!' Pixie railed at him, frantically trying to get out of the other side of the car only to be foiled by the automatic locks. 'Let me out!'

'No,' Apollo decreed, temper moderated by the simple fact that he had her back again where she should be. 'You shouldn't have let him touch you like that.'

'Are you for real?' Pixie screamed at him. 'You've had women throwing themselves at you and pawing you all evening!'

Apollo shot her a riveting green glance of near wonderment. 'That approach works on other women...what's wrong with you?'

'What's *right* with me is that I'm not about to let you walk all over me!' Pixie hissed back. 'Anything you can do I can do too and I will. I'll throw myself at every man in my radius if it annoys you enough... I hate you, Apollo... I *hate* you!'

Apollo watched her stalk like a miniature warrior onto the motorboat and sit down as far as she could get from him. Marriage promised to be a great deal more challenging than he had ever appreciated, he conceded, still lightheaded from the sheer amount of rage that had flooded him when he'd seen the Prince put his hands on her. How dared he? He gritted his even white teeth while he fought the lingering pulses of fury.

With a flourish intended to convey sarcasm, Pixie whipped off her shoes before she boarded the yacht. 'And we abandoned our guests on our night out,' she remarked in a stinging tone. 'Some hosts we make.'

'If you think Holly and Vito want to come back and find themselves in the middle of a marital spat, you're mental. They'll stay out until dawn,' Apollo forecast, grim-mouthed.

CHAPTER EIGHT

PIXIE SLUNG HER shoes across their stateroom in a gesture of frustrated fury. Apollo had acted like a total ass all evening and then somehow made a fool of her as if *she* were the one in the wrong? How was that fair? How was she supposed to forgive him for that? How was she supposed to cope with being married to such a maniac? So much for the business arrangement!

The door clicked open and Pixie spun. 'I'm not sleeping in here with you tonight.'

Apollo simply depressed the lock and studied her. 'You're not sleeping anyplace else.'

'You've got *ten* guest cabins. What is the matter with you?' Pixie exclaimed furiously. 'What do you want from me?'

Apollo surveyed her steadily, concealing his growing bewilderment at his own actions with difficulty. He had lost his head and he didn't ever do that.

'Are you going to answer me?' Pixie asked impatiently, one hand planted on her hip while her foot tapped cheekily on the floor.

He just wanted her. Somehow she was like a missing puzzle piece he had to have at any price. The sex had been amazing. It was the fireworks and the sex that attracted him. She was having the weirdest effect on him. Problem solved and sorted, he told himself stubbornly.

'Any time soon?' Pixie prodded in frustration. 'Like… tonight?'

Apollo unbuttoned his shirt for want of anything better to do. A knock sounded on the door and he answered it. Hector raced in, paused in horror at the sight of Apollo, gave him a very wide berth and shot trembling below the bed. Apollo locked the door again. 'You're my wife,' he told her finally, and as far as he was concerned at that moment that covered everything he needed to say.

Pixie was perplexed by that response. 'But not a real wife…'

'We're legally married, having sex and I'm trying to get you pregnant. How could it be any *more* real?' Apollo enquired. 'Tonight I felt married.'

Her smooth brow indented, grey eyes shimmering with indignation. 'Well, if that's how you behave when you're married, I wouldn't like to have been around when you were still single.'

'I wasn't expecting you to hit back,' he admitted with startling abruptness, his beautiful wilful mouth curling with a sudden amusement that enraged her even more. 'Clever move, *koukla mou*. Guaranteed to get a rise out of a guy as basic as me.'

Her breasts swelled temptingly over the top of the corset as she breathed in very, very deeply. 'You think it was some kind of strategy to get your attention back?' she shouted at him in disbelief.

'It worked,' Apollo pointed out drily. 'So, presumably it was deliberate?'

'No, it freakin' well wasn't deliberate!' Pixie launched at him, bending to scoop up a shoe and hurl it at him in furious rebuttal of that conviction. 'How dare you be so big-headed that you can think that?'

'I'll let it go this once,' Apollo murmured silkily. 'But if you ever let another guy touch you like that again you'll pay for it.'

'Threatening violence now?' Pixie questioned, scooping the other shoe and holding it like a weapon.

'No, you're rather more violent than I am. You've already punched me once and now you're throwing stuff at me,' Apollo pointed out deadpan.

Pixie threw the second shoe but he was quick on his feet and she missed. Hector started to whine below the bed.

'I can allow you to do a lot of things I haven't allowed a woman to do before, *koukla mou*,' Apollo intoned as he strode forward, 'but I really can't stand by and allow you to frighten that dog!'

Hauling her up into his arms, Apollo sat down on the bed. 'Settle down,' he instructed, pinning an arm round her to stop hers from flailing. 'You've got my full attention.'

'And now I don't *want* it!' Pixie yelled at him, so wound up with emotion she almost felt tearful over her inability to express herself.

'I'm afraid you're stuck with it,' Apollo told her, dropping his arm to frame her face with big controlling hands. 'I want you.'

'No!' Pixie snapped, striving to clamber off him again.

'You want me too, you just won't admit it,' Apollo opined in frustration.

'Do you ever listen to yourself? Marvel at the little megalomaniac remarks you make?'

His beautiful stubborn mouth claimed hers in a scorching kiss and her temperature rose like a rocket.

She felt hot, she felt faint, she spread her hands against his shoulders and, meeting shirt fabric, slid her fingers beneath the parted edges to find warm brown skin. His tongue dipped and plunged and one of her hands delved into his luxuriant black hair. As she knelt over him, he pushed up her skirt and ground her hips down on him. Suddenly she was achingly aware of the long hard thrust of him behind his zip. Liquid warmth surged between her thighs and she gasped, her nipples swelling and tightening. Yanking down the zip on her top, Apollo cast it aside and bent her slender body back over one arm to suck at a pretty pouting nipple, a manoeuvre that dragged an agonised moan from low in her throat.

'I'm not speaking to you!' Pixie exclaimed in consternation.

'Since when was speech required?' Apollo groaned, reaching with difficulty below her skirt to rip at the fragile lace of her panties and then touch her with frighteningly knowing fingers in the exact spot she could least resist.

'Apollo!' Pixie muttered furiously, helpless in the grip of the sensations flooding her and blaming him for the fact.

He met her shaken eyes and he smiled with sudden brilliance. 'I want you much more than I've ever wanted any other woman,' he breathed in a raw and shaken undertone.

Oh, the combination of that smile and those tantalising words, it left Pixie dizzy and without her conscious volition her arms slid round his neck and she leant against him, momentarily hiding her face, her thoughts in a messy whirl. *What's wrong with me? Why do I still want him? What happened to the anger?*

Lifting her head, she clashed with black-lashed gorgeous green and her heart gave a hop, skip and a jump as though he had hit a switch. And she told herself she couldn't *possibly* be falling for him. No, she was too sensible and not at all the type who would build herself up knowing she would only be broken down by the end of the relationship. It was lust, wild, wicked lust, and it was merely hitting her harder because she was a late developer.

Apollo stroked her, teased her tingling core, reducing her defences to forgotten rubble until all she wanted, all she craved, was for the ravaging, greedy hunger to be sated. He tipped her back, removed the tight skirt to the accompaniment of a ripping sound that implied damage, unzipped and came down on her without even undressing. 'Can't wait,' he growled. 'Have to have you now.'

He pushed into her with scant ceremony but that hard, driving fullness was absolutely what her body needed and desired just then. A cry of compliance left her lips, followed by an ecstatic sigh of gratification when he moved. He changed position to hit her at another angle and she jerked and moaned with pleasure, hearing herself, inwardly cringing for herself but wanting him and that feeling so powerfully she couldn't fight her own hunger. The waves of pleasure rolled faster and faster, the sensual power of him overwhelming. Her climax engulfed her like an avalanche driving all before it, emptying her of thought, breaking her down into a blissful bundle of pure satisfaction. In the aftermath she was weighted to the bed by Apollo and she decided she might never want to move again.

He scooped her up and slotted her into bed, kneeling over her to almost frantically wrench himself out of what remained of his clothing. That achieved, he crushed her mouth under his again. 'Hope you're not tired,' he breathed in a driven undertone. 'I think I could go all night...'

They were at peace again. Apollo told himself that that had been his ultimate goal but he already knew that what he craved most was the joy of sinking into her honeyed depths again. There was simply something about her, something that acted on him like an aphrodisiac. He wasn't going to think about it. Why should he? What was the point? Fabulous sex didn't need to be dissected: it simply *was*. Gritting his teeth, he slowly edged an arm round her and she didn't need much of an invitation after that. In fact she scooted across the divide between them and clamped to the side of him like a landmine, doing all the work for him, he conceded in relief.

'Women like hugs,' Vito had told him as if it were some great secret known only to the precious few. Apollo didn't like hugging women but he believed he could learn to pretend that he did...particularly if it encouraged sex, he reflected with a sudden wolfish grin. *Be nice,* Holly had told him without much apparent hope that he could possibly deliver on that suggestion.

But when it came to strategy, Apollo was very much on a level with Vito in business. He had misjudged his audience when he'd waited for Pixie to throw a jealous scene at the club, had actually felt pretty offended when she'd failed to deliver on that front but he wouldn't make that mistake again. No, he would listen and observe and learn until their marriage became much more civilised and both of them got what they wanted out of the arrangement. That was the rational approach and designed to provide the most desirable result, he reasoned with satisfaction.

While Apollo was deliberating with what he believed to be perfect rationality, Pixie was feeling as irrational as a bunch of dandelion seeds left to blow hither and thither in the wind. She had no guidance, no foundation stone for the strong feelings that assailed her when Apollo, apparently quite naturally, wrapped both arms tightly around her. He made her feel safe. He made her feel as if he cared. He made her feel as if she was indeed special. And even though the common sense in her hind brain was already sneering that she was nothing in comparison with the leggy, glamorous underwear models of the type he favoured, she was happy for the first time in a long time, happy instead of just getting through the day...

She decided she wasn't going to waste energy worrying or picking herself apart with self-loathing criticisms. He was right on one thing: she wanted *him*. And if their marriage was to work on any level they had to have that chemistry and use it accordingly. A lean hand smoothed down her spine and she quivered and stopped thinking altogether.

Apollo had already laid the trail and Hector was becoming an old hand at following treat trails.

The scruffy little animal crept out from his roofed hidey hole of a basket and snuffled up the treats, inching half under Apollo's desk while Apollo pretended to ignore his progress. Every week the little terrier dared to move a little closer to the male who terrified him—not that Apollo took that personally. Hector was uniformly terrified of every man that came into his vicinity and considerably more trusting of the female sex. He had first bonded with Pixie in the vet surgery where his injuries had been tended. Pixie had worked next door and, being friendly with the veterinary nurse, had often visited the homeless dogs in their cages. Although Pixie had worked and did not have a garden, the vet had deemed her a good prospective owner because Hector had taken to her immediately.

At least, though, Hector was rather more predictable than Pixie, Apollo conceded with a frown.

He could see that Pixie didn't really trust anything he said. It was as if she was fully convinced that he could never be anything other than a womaniser, as if she believed he carried some genetic flaw that made him unsuitable for any other purpose, and it was quietly driving him crazy. He had never met a woman so resistant to his attempts to change her mind about him. In bed, she was his perfect match, the only woman he had ever met as highly sexed as he was, but beyond that bedroom door she was blind to his best efforts. He tossed a squeaky toy across the desk in Hector's direction. He was expecting the dog to run away from it but Hector took him by surprise and pounced with apparent glee on the toy and pummelled it with his paws, seemingly pleased by the frantic squeaking that resulted.

Pixie stretched a daring toe out of the bed and slowly sat up, checking her newly unreliable body for the roiling wave of sickness that had attacked her on several occasions throughout the week. Even though she stood up equally slowly, that was still when the nausea hit and with a groan she raced for the bathroom. After a shower she got dressed, her stomach restored to normality again. Was she pregnant? If she was, she could only be at a very early stage and she doubted that she could already be suffering from nausea. Her hopes, after all, had been dashed after the first couple of weeks of their marriage passed and her cycle kicked in as normal. It had seemed incredible to her even then that all that sex hadn't led straight to conception. This time, however, her period was a little late but not late enough to risk raising false hopes, so she had said nothing to Apollo as yet.

A false alarm would be embarrassing but what was really bothering her was the disturbing suspicion that even if she *had* conceived she still wouldn't want to rush into telling him. And why would that be?

Pixie coloured as she pulled on shorts and a tee and then dried her hair. No, she still wasn't using the on-board beauty salon for that because she had always liked doing her own hair. She was using it for other services though, she conceded, glancing at her perfectly manicured nails and equally well-groomed brows. Apollo's wealthy lifestyle was slowly but surely overtaking the former ordinary informality of hers. It scared her to accept that she was becoming accustomed to wearing designer clothes and expensive jewellery. Apollo called it 'looking the part' and she had to agree that nobody would take their marriage seriously if she went around dressed like a beggar or a bag lady. But even so, sometimes she felt as though she was losing an essential part of herself and that would have to be her independence.

Of course, everything would change if she *was* pregnant, she told herself unhappily. Apollo would reclaim his previous life and return happily to acting like the biggest man whore in Europe. After all, once a pregnancy was achieved there would be no reason for him to stay with Pixie or settle for having only one woman in his life. There wouldn't even be a reason for him to share a bed with her any longer…it would be the effective end of their supposed marriage.

And there it was. The sad truth that lay at the heart of her anxieties. She was hopelessly in love with a husband who wasn't a real husband. She had learned so much about Apollo over the past six weeks and he was not at all like the playboy he was depicted as in the tabloids and on the gossip sites on the Internet. She had always wondered why he and Vito, who was rather serious in nature, were such close friends when at first glance as men they were so very unalike. And in temperament, family background and outlook they *were* very different but not anything like as different as Pixie had originally assumed.

Apollo supported loads of charities and the main one, she had discovered, was a charity for abused children. But the charitable cause possibly closest to his heart was an abandoned pets' sanctuary he had set up in Athens. On the Metraxis island of Nexos he had also established a therapy centre where the more damaged animals were rehabilitated and she couldn't wait to visit it and possibly pick up a few tips from the professionals there on how best to handle Hector's fear. It was hard facts of that nature that had begun to eradicate Pixie's former hostile distrust of Apollo.

Ever since that evening at the nightclub when they had both lost their tempers, the mood had changed between them. They had not been apart for even a night since then. Pixie's mouth quirked. She wasn't sure Apollo could get by one night without sex. Or that she could. Indeed the stormy fizzing passion they shared in bed thrilled her almost as much as it could still unnerve her. Naturally they still fought on occasion but in every way their relationship seemed so normal that it was a continual battle for Pixie to remember that their marriage wasn't really a marriage at all, but a business arrangement with the ultimate goal of conception and a very firm end date.

Her brother, Patrick, however, wasn't aware of those facts and brother and sister talked regularly on the phone. Since the wedding her brother had become more honest, finally admitting that he did have a problem with gambling. Patrick was now seeing an addiction counsellor and attending Gamblers Anonymous on a regular basis. Although Pixie had been furious when she'd realised that Apollo had confronted her brother about his issues without consulting her, she had changed her mind on that score, deciding that even though she hadn't liked Apollo's methods his approach had been the right one. After all, but for Apollo's intervention she wouldn't even have known that her sibling was still gambling. Furthermore, given advice and support, Patrick now had a much better chance of overcoming his gambling dependency and living a happier and much safer life.

It probably wasn't even slightly surprising that she had fallen so hard for Apollo, Pixie reflected ruefully. He was her first lover, her first *everything* and like any legendary stud he had buckets of charisma when he tried to impress. And that was what she couldn't afford to forget, Pixie reminded herself doggedly: Apollo was *faking* it for her benefit and his. Did he think that she was so stupid that she didn't know that?

Obviously every seemingly concerned or pleasant thing he had done around her was a giant fake!

After all, the stress and strain of a bad relationship could prevent her from getting pregnant while simple strife would keep her out of his bed. So, when she had dived off the top deck of *Circe* to surprise him because she was a very proficient swimmer and diver and Apollo had gone ballistic at the supposed dangerous risk he had deemed her to have taken, his evident concern for what might have happened to her couldn't possibly have been genuine. If she killed herself diving it would be inconvenient for him but with his resources and attraction he would quickly replace her, Pixie thought, miserably melodramatic in the mood she was in.

In the same way, the many trips they had shared, stopping off to swim and picnic in secluded coves and explore enchanting little villages on various Greek islands were not to be taken too seriously. Apollo enjoyed showing off the beauties of his homeland and was a great deal better educated than she had initially appreciated. She had discovered that he could give her chapter and verse on every ancient Greek or Roman site they came on. Her fingers fiddled restively with the little gold and diamond tiger pendant she wore. He had given her that a week after that nightclub scene, telling her that she was much more than a kitten with claws. Since she had scored his back in the heat of passion with her nails the night before he had given it to her she had laughed in appreciation. And that had annoyed Apollo, something she seemed to do sometimes without even meaning to, she acknowledged with regret.

But then, undeniably, Apollo was mercurial and volatile, passionate and outspoken and still in many ways a mystery and a contradiction to Pixie. He was a billionaire with every luxury at his command and yet he could picnic on a beach quite happily with a rough bottle of the village vino, home-baked bread and a salad scattered with the salty local cheese. He clearly loved dogs and could have owned a select pack of pedigreed animals without any need of therapy, but he had not owned a dog since childhood and seemed to prefer to spend his time trying to win Hector's trust. And Hector was the most ordinary of ordinary little terriers with the scrappy stubborn nature of his breed and he was extremely reluctant to change his defensive habits.

The door opened and Pixie scrambled up as her dog trailed after Apollo into the room. Hector wouldn't go *to* Apollo but he was quite happy to follow him at a safe distance. Clad in tailored chino pants and an open-necked black shirt, Apollo slanted her a reproving grin. 'What's with all this sleeping in every morning? You didn't join me for breakfast again,' he complained.

'Maybe you're wearing me out,' Pixie quipped.

His green eyes gleamed like jewels fringed by lush black lashes in his lean, strong face. 'Am I too demanding?' he suddenly asked with a frown.

And Pixie went pink, dismay assailing her because she had been teasing. 'No more than I am,' she muttered, her eyes veiling as she remembered wakening him up at some time of the night and taking thorough advantage of his lean, hard body to satisfy the need that never entirely receded in his radius.

Apollo wrapped a careless arm round her shoulders. 'I do like an honest woman,' he confessed with husky sensual recollection.

'No, what you like is being my only object of desire,' Pixie corrected, her body sliding into the lean, hard embrace of his as if it were programmed to do so.

He bent his dark head and claimed her bee-stung mouth with a hungry thoroughness that tightened her nipples and ran like fire to the heart of her and she trembled against his hard, muscular frame, suddenly weak again in a way she hated. She denied herself the desire to put her arms round him. She didn't want Apollo to know how she felt about him because that would inevitably make their relationship uncomfortable. Hadn't she promised him that she wouldn't turn clingy or needy? And that she had no intention of falling for him? Even worse, she thought painfully, she had truly believed she could deliver on those pledges of faith in his undesirability.

Her incredibly tender breasts ached with a mixture of oversensitivity and swelling desire when he crushed her to him with sudden force and for a split second she knew he could have done anything he wanted with her because she had no resistance and no longer any defences to fall back on to support her.

It was disconcerting when Apollo set her back from him in an uncharacteristic move of restraint. 'No,' he breathed in a fractured undertone. 'I came down to bring you up on deck. I want you to see the island for the first time as we come into harbour.'

And Pixie understood why he had backed off even though it did make her feel a little like an overdose of sugar being rejected by someone who had decided to go on a diet. In truth she had always accepted, she thought ruefully, that Apollo *could* resist her if he chose to do so and naturally that hurt her pride and her heart, but it was also a fact of life she had better learn to live with. After all, if she had already conceived she suspected their actual future as a couple could be measured in days rather than months.

Furthermore, the island of Nexos, the home of the Metraxis family for several generations, was hugely important to Apollo and probably one of the main reasons he had married her. Without a wife and a child he could not securely claim his heritage.

Pixie stood out on deck with the bright blue sky above her and the sun beating down while *Circe* powered more slowly than usual towards the island spread before them. Apollo slid his arms round her from behind and she leant back against him to be more comfortable, her keen and curious gaze scanning the pine trees edging the sandy beach at one end of the island and the rocky cliffs towering at the other. In the middle there was greenery and silvery olive groves and a fair-sized village climbing the hill behind the harbour—little white cube houses stretching in all directions while a little domed stone church presided over the flat land at the water's edge.

'It's beautiful,' she murmured dreamily.

'I didn't properly appreciate Nexos as my home until I thought about losing it,' Apollo intoned grimly. 'If I'd confided more in my father he would not have left that will as his final testament to me.'

'It doesn't matter now, not really,' Pixie reasoned, hopelessly eager to provide comfort when she recognised the emotional undertow of regret in his dark deep drawl. 'Maybe your father simply knew what bait to put on the hook.'

Apollo burst out laughing without the smallest warning and gazed down at the top of her golden head. 'I doubt if he appreciated you would be less than five foot tall and a hairdresser. A talented one though, I must admit, *koukla mou*,' he added, clearly worried that he had hurt her feelings and that she had interpreted that reminder of her more humble beginnings as a put-down. 'As bait you have proved as efficient as a torpedo under the water line.'

Destructive? Was that how he saw her? Was that because he had confided in her about his evil stepmothers? Or because he had shown her that he was as vulnerable as any other human being in childhood? And as amazingly loveable, she conceded wretchedly, worry dragging her down again along with the fear of the separation she saw waiting on the horizon.

CHAPTER NINE

'YOU SHOULD CHANGE before we disembark,' Apollo urged. 'The press will be waiting at the harbour.'

'The *press*?' Pixie emphasised, eyes flying wide. 'Why would they be waiting?'

'I issued a press release about our marriage last week,' Apollo admitted. 'They'll want a photo since I saw no reason to be that generous.'

'I thought Nexos was a private island,' Pixie admitted tautly, disconcerted at the prospect of camera lenses being trained on her for she had yet to be photographed in Apollo's company. That was undoubtedly because Apollo hated the paparazzi and knew exactly where to go to avoid attracting that kind of attention.

'It is but not as private as it was in my grandfather's day. The islanders need to make a living and my father began letting tourists in twenty years ago. I accelerated that process by building an eco-resort on the other side of the island,' he revealed calmly. 'The years of the locals getting by fishing and farming are long gone. Not unnaturally their children want more.'

'And even if that infringes on your privacy on your island you let them have it,' Pixie remarked in surprise.

'It doesn't infringe. The Metraxis estate is very secure but owning an island with an indigenous population comes with responsibility. The people have to have a future they can count on for their children or the younger generation will leave. My father didn't really grasp that reality.'

Pixie stepped into the motor launch twenty minutes later, clad in print silk trousers with a toning shirt worn over a camisole and a sunhat that she had to hang onto as the launch sped across the gleaming clear turquoise water into the harbour. She tensed when she saw just how many people seemed to be grouped there ready to greet them. It dawned on her that in her guise as Apollo's wife she probably seemed a much more important person to the locals than she actually was.

'Don't answer any questions whatsoever. Ignore the cameras,' Apollo urged, lifting her into his arms to carry her off the launch before she could make for the steps under her own steam.

Flushed and uneasy, Pixie regained her feet and Apollo's bodyguards swung into action to keep the photographers at a careful distance. With the indolent cool of a male accustomed to the press invading his privacy, Apollo dropped an arm round her shoulders and walked her off the marina at an unhurried pace. He exchanged greetings in his own language with several people but he did not once pause in his determined progress towards the four-wheel drive parked in readiness beyond the crush.

Pixie, however, had never been so uneasily conscious of being the centre of attention and she was hopelessly intimidated by the shouted questions and comments in different languages. She felt the wall of stares being directed at her and her tummy gave a sick lurch. She suspected that she had to be a pretty disappointing spectacle for people who had probably expected Apollo to marry an heiress or a model and, at the very least, someone famous, incredibly beautiful and photogenic. Possessing none of those gifts, she felt horribly exposed and all the more aware that she was a fake wife, pregnant or otherwise.

Only when they were inside the car did she breathe again.

'See…that wasn't so bad,' Apollo pointed out with a shrug that perfectly illustrated his indifference to that amount of concentrated interest and speculation.

'I'll take your word for it… I found it tough,' Pixie responded honestly. 'I'm not used to being looked at like that and knowing I am a totally phony wife doesn't add to my confidence.'

'When will you listen to me?' Apollo shot back at her in exasperation. 'You're my *legal* wife!'

Pixie breathed in slow and deep to calm her racing nerves and turned her head to look out of the car windows. Apollo had taught her that a legal wife still wasn't a *real* wife.

'And you will never leave our estate without bodyguards…is that understood? Not even for a walk down into the village,' Apollo specified.

'Is that level of security really necessary?' 'Our' estate, he had said, she noted in surprise, and then wrote it off as either a slip of the tongue or a comment designed to make her feel more relaxed about their living arrangements.

'There's always a risk of paparazzi in the village or even a tourist photographing you to make a profit. My security team are trained to handle all that and ensure that nobody gets to bother you.'

The car was travelling up a steep incline and electric gates whirred back while Pixie gazed at the big white rambling villa at the top of the hill. It was certainly large but it wasn't anywhere near as massive as Vito's giant palazzo in Tuscany and she was relieved. As she stepped out, one of the bodyguards lifted Hector's carrier from the four-wheel drive and set it down to release him. Hector raced out and gambolled round Pixie's ankles, relieved to have escaped his brief imprisonment.

They walked into a grand marble-floored space with staircases sweeping down on either side of the hall and a very opulent chandelier. A housekeeper, dressed in black with a white apron, greeted them and was introduced as Olympia. Apollo spoke to her at length in Greek while Pixie succumbed to curiosity and crossed the hall to peep into rooms. She had never seen so many dead white walls in her life or such bland furnishings. Indeed the interior had the appearance of a house that served as a show home.

Apollo frowned as he examined her expressive face. 'You don't like it? Then you can change it. I had it all stripped, painted and refurnished while my father was ill. Every one of his wives had different decorating ideas and favourite rooms and the house was a mess of clashing colours and styles. When he was well enough to come down for dinner I realised that the décor awakened unfortunate memories so I wiped the slate clean for his benefit.'

'Well, all that white and beige is certainly clean,' Pixie assured him gently, rather touched by his thoughtfulness on his ailing father's behalf.

'I'll show you round,' he proffered, walking her from room to room, and there really was very little to look at in the big colourless rooms. There were no photographs, no ornaments, only an occasional vase of beautiful flowers.

'I thought the house would be much larger,' she confided as he walked her upstairs. 'Holly said you had a lot of relatives.'

'Relatives and friends use the guest cottages behind

the house. My grandfather and my father preferred to have only family members lodge in the actual house. Vito and Holly stayed here with me for the funeral because Vito is the closest thing I have to a brother,' he admitted quietly, his handsome mouth quirking. 'But don't go repeating that or he'll get too big for his boots.'

Pixie laughed as he showed her into a spacious bedroom with a balcony running the entire length. The pale curtains beside the open doors streamed back in the breeze coming in off the ocean. She stepped outside to appreciate the incredible bird's eye view of Nexos and the sea and understood exactly why Apollo's grandfather had chosen that spot to build his family home. 'It is really gorgeous,' she murmured. 'But this place could definitely do with some pictures on the walls and other stuff just to take the bare look away.'

'The canvases are stored in the basement but run it by me before you have anything rehung,' Apollo countered. 'There are portraits of the ex-wives, which I have no desire to see again…and certain artworks fall into the same category,' he completed tight-mouthed.

Pixie rested a tiny hand on his. 'This is your home. The ex-wives are gone now and won't be coming back, so forget about them.'

Apollo bit out an embittered laugh. 'Only if I contrive to produce a child…and who knows whether or not that will be possible?'

Pixie pinned her lips together and stared out to sea and then she couldn't hold the words bubbling on her tongue back any longer. 'There may be a slim chance that this month…well, don't go getting excited yet *but* I am a little late…'

Apollo stared down at her transfixed by even the slender possibility that she had outlined. 'And you didn't even mention it to me until now?' he demanded in seething disbelief.

'Because we don't need to put ourselves through some silly false alarm, do we?' Pixie appealed.

Apollo shook his head as if he couldn't identify with that attitude. His black hair blew back from his lean bronzed features as he leant back against the glass barrier, his green eyes jewel bright in the sunlight. He dug out his phone, stabbed buttons with impatience and started talking in fast Greek while she watched, frowning in bewilderment.

'Dr Floros will come up with a test for us this afternoon.'

'But I'm only a couple of days late,' Pixie protested.

'Even *I* know that that's usually soon enough to tell us one way or the other,' Apollo pronounced. 'Why sit around wondering any longer?'

Well, you chose to open your big mouth and spill, Pixie censured herself unhappily. He would either be very pleased or very disappointed. It was out of her hands now.

'You have to learn the habit of *sharing* these things with me,' Apollo breathed in an almost raw undertone, green eyes veiled and narrowed as he stared down at her.

'Didn't I just do that?'

'Obviously you've been thinking about this on your own for a few days and that's not how I want you to behave, *koukla mou.* The minute anything worries you bring it to me.'

But even as Apollo gazed down at Pixie, his big frame was stiffening and he was losing colour because ill-starred memories were being stirred up by their predicament. He had quite deliberately closed out the awareness that sometimes women died in childbirth: his mother had. More than once his father, Vassilis had discussed that tragedy with his son. Vassilis had idolised Apollo's mother and he had never really come to terms with losing her in such terrible circumstances. At the moment when he should have been happiest with his wife and his newborn child he had been plunged into grief.

'What's wrong?' Pixie asked abruptly, watching sharp tension tighten the sculpted lines of Apollo's lean, hard face.

'Nothing. I forgot,' Apollo said equally abruptly, 'I have a couple of work calls to make. Will you be all right settling in here on your own?'

'Of course I will be.'

Apollo strode down the stairs like a hungry lion in search of prey. If Pixie was pregnant, there would be no home birth, he reasoned with immediate resolve. No, she was going to a fully equipped hospital regardless of how she felt about that decision. He would also engage a standby medical team. He wouldn't take any risks with her because he was too conscious that something quite unexpected could happen during a birth. He wouldn't mention that to Pixie though. He wasn't that stupid. He didn't want her worrying and certainly not to the extent *he* was suddenly worrying.

For a split second he was grudgingly amused by his own attitude. He had married Pixie to have a child and now that there was a chance they might have succeeded at step one, he was suddenly awash with anxiety. She was so small...and the baby could be big as he had been... and now he needed a drink.

By the time Pixie had watched her luggage being unpacked, enjoyed a cup of tea on the shaded terrace alone and even taken Hector for a walk through the meandering gardens with tree-lined paths alone, she had accepted that Apollo was not as excited by the concept of becoming a father as she was excited about becoming a mother. He had vanished like Scotch mist and she felt that they did not have the kind of marriage that empowered her to go looking for him as a normal wife might have done. Looking for Apollo any place struck Pixie as clingy and she refused to act clingy.

Dr Floros arrived, middle-aged and bearded and relentlessly cheerful even in the face of Apollo's grave demeanour. Yes, Apollo had finally reappeared and Pixie could not help but notice that her husband was as grim as a pall-bearer in comparison to the chirpy medical man. Maybe the actual prospect of a child was a little sobering for a playboy, Pixie reasoned uncertainly as she took the test and vanished into the palatial cloakroom on the ground floor. It would be foolish of her to think that he had lost his original enthusiasm for conception. That wasn't possible, was it?

'My wife is very small in size,' Apollo remarked to the doctor while Pixie was absent.

'Nature has a wonderful way of taking such differences into account,' Dr Floros assured him without concern. 'I'll take a blood test as well if the result is positive.'

Pixie watched the test wand change colour, but since the packaging and instructions were in Greek she had no idea what was a positive and what was a negative and had to return in continuing ignorance to the two men.

Dr Floros beamed before she even reached them. 'Congratulations!' he pronounced in English.

Pixie felt a little dizzy at the confirmation that she was going to be a mother and she sat down hurriedly, her attention locked to Apollo's lean, strong face. He froze, betraying nothing, neither smiling nor even wincing in reaction and she wanted to slap him for it. Apollo

explained about the blood test and Pixie stood up a lit-
tle nervously because she didn't like needles. Indeed Dr
Floros only got as far as flourishing his syringe before
Pixie felt faint, her knees wobbling so obviously that
Apollo gripped her to steady her.

'Are you all right?'

And no, she wasn't all right because at that point she
fainted and resurfaced lying on a sofa.

'Don't look at the needle...' Apollo urged, quick as always to identify the source of her fear, and he crouched
down beside her and held her hand as tightly as if she
were drowning.

The test was done. She apologised to the doctor and
he said it was probably the combination of the good news
and stress that had made her pass out. Dr Floros departed and Apollo reappeared with Olympia carrying
a pot of tea.

'You could say something now,' Pixie prompted when
they were finally alone.

Apollo frowned. 'About what?'

'Well, it did only take us six weeks...you could look
happy, look *pleased*!' Pixie emphasised in annoyance.

'I am pleased,' Apollo assured her unconvincingly.
'But not if it makes you ill and you collapse like that.
That was scary.'

'I didn't exactly enjoy it. I hate needles and injections
and I felt so dizzy and then everything went dark,' Pixie
explained rather curtly. 'I'm not about to be ill. I'm simply pregnant and there are a few symptoms that come
with that. Dizziness is one of them. Holly was always
getting light-headed.'

'Luckily we have a lift, so you won't have to use the
stairs.'

Pixie studied him in wonderment. 'You expect me to use a lift to go up or down one floor? Are you crazy?'

'You could *fall* on the stairs,' Apollo traded with deadly seriousness.

'Thank you, Mr Cheerful.' Pixie rested her head back and tried to imagine becoming a mother. She wasn't about to let Apollo's strange lack of enthusiasm take the edge off her sense of joy and achievement. A baby, a darling, gorgeous little baby who was hers *and* his. She couldn't keep Apollo but she *could* keep their baby. She was happy, really, really happy about that aspect and suspected it would be something of a comfort in the future when Apollo was no longer a constant part of her life.

There would be a divorce first, she reminded herself doggedly. Then she would have to get accustomed to seeing him with other women in tabloid pictures, knowing he was sharing a bed with them while also knowing exactly what he was doing with them there. Doubtless he would phone her to keep up to date with their child's development and from time to time he would visit in person until the child was old enough to go and visit him. It would all be very civilised and polite but she was already painfully aware that losing Apollo would smash her heart to smithereens!

Apollo studied the tears rolling down Pixie's cheeks as she stared up at the ceiling. She wasn't happy about being pregnant and he wondered why he had expected otherwise. She liked kids, he knew she did, but then they weren't having a child in the most ideal circumstances, he reminded himself grimly. She was having a child she would pretty much raise alone and possibly she felt trapped because at her age most women were young, single and free as the air.

A chilling shot of rage assailed Apollo at the image of

Pixie reclaiming her freedom after a divorce and becoming intimate with another man. He had the strangest possessive feelings where she was concerned, he conceded in bemusement. For some reason too he was feeling as exhausted as if he had climbed a mountain. Somehow Pixie being pregnant was incredibly stressful. No, worse than stressful, *frightening*, he adjusted in consternation. For the first time it occurred to him that Vito had been saved from such concerns by only entering his son Angelo's life when the baby was already six months old. Was it normal for a first-time father to feel on the edge of panic? He crushed the reaction and went into denial.

'By the way, we're having a big party here in a few weeks,' Apollo announced in a determined change of subject. 'I organised it last month.'

'Thanks for sharing *after* the event,' Pixie said sarcastically.

'I've invited friends and family here to celebrate our marriage but I didn't fancy a wedding-type event,' Apollo confided with a cynical twist of his mouth. 'I settled on a fancy-dress party for a theme.'

'Oh, joy...' Pixie mumbled sleepily as she turned her face into a cushion, presenting him with her narrow back.

'I've taken care of our outfits,' Apollo told her with pride, relieved she would not be put to the worry of wondering what she should wear and very much hoping that she would appreciate the amount of trouble he had gone to.

'Your way or the highway,' Pixie whispered unappreciatively. 'Don't worry. I knew what a control freak you were the day I married you.'

Apollo surveyed Hector, who was seated on the rug, his little face seemingly anxious. *You and me too, buddy,* Apollo thought wryly while he wondered if it was possible that Pixie could roll off the sofa and hurt herself while she slept. For the first time in his life concern was weighing him down like a big grey cloud closing out the sun. He had never truly had to worry about anyone but his father but now he had a wife and a child on the way. He thought it extraordinary that achieving the pregnancy required to fulfil the terms of his father's will should suddenly and quite inexplicably feel, not like a prize, but more like a poisoned chalice.

Apollo came to bed in the early hours. Having persuaded herself that he might not even choose to still share the same room, Pixie was lying sleepless watching the moonlight glimmer through the shadows. She listened to him in the shower, watched him stride naked towards the bed and sensual heat curled low in her body because she could see that he was aroused.

Apollo slid quietly into bed and lay there, thoroughly irritated by the throbbing at his groin. Pixie was pregnant, fragile and definitely *off-limits*. But it was as if she had lit a fire in him the first time they had had sex. It was a fire only she could seem to cool and that knowledge seriously disturbed him. Throughout his adult life Apollo had viewed sex as a casual diversion from more important activities. Sex had always been easily available and his libido had never homed in on one particular woman. His life had been wonderfully simple, he reflected grimly. He would see a woman he wanted, enjoy her for a while and when he got bored move on to the next. And now, for some peculiar reason, he wasn't getting bored any more…and he was feeling urges he had no desire to feel.

Pixie shifted across the bed inch by inch, wishing it weren't quite so big. Her hand settled on the male shoulder furthest from her and slowly drifted down over Apollo's magnificent torso. She smiled as she felt his hard muscles ripple and tense across his abdomen.

He turned towards her and his eyes glittered in the moonlight. 'We shouldn't,' he breathed with sudden amusement.

'Don't be silly,' Pixie whispered, her tiny hand heading further south to find the long, jutting length of him and stroke. 'I'm pregnant, not breakable.'

Apollo groaned out loud and arched his lean hips while watching her slide below the sheet to administer an even more potent invitation and that fast his once renowned self-control broke like a dam breaking its banks. He tugged Pixie up to him with shuddering impatience and rolled her under him while his hungry mouth tasted hers with heated urgency.

'That's more like it,' Pixie commented a shade smugly as she gazed up at him, her fingers skimming caressingly through his damp, tousled hair. She felt lighter than air at the ego-boosting confirmation that he still wanted her. Intelligence warned her that he was a young healthy male, who was usually in the mood for sex, but she refused to think about that angle, choosing to concentrate instead on the soothing conviction that pregnancy wasn't quite the turn-off she had feared.

'There is only one way this can continue,' Apollo decreed, resting her back against the pillows. 'You lie there... *I* do the work, *koukla mou.*'

And it was amazing, she thought much later, drifting into an exhausted and gratified sleep, but then it always was amazing with Apollo.

Apollo held her while she slept and marvelled at how natural it had become to hold her close. One large hand splayed across her flat stomach. How had he ever believed that he could walk away untouched after conception occurred? How had he credited that he could bring a child into the world and not want to play a full part in his son or daughter's life? The unquestioning arrogance of those selfish assumptions belatedly savaged his view of himself. As fond memories of moments with his own father while he was still a little boy drifted through his mind he finally understood Vassilis Metraxis's almost primitive need to safeguard the continuation of the family line, and he also grasped that walking away at any stage from his own child wasn't an option he would ever be able to live with.

CHAPTER TEN

THREE WEEKS LATER, Pixie blinked sleepily into wakeful-
ness and finally sat up to make a grab for the phone ringing while ruefully contemplating the empty space beside
her. It was forty-eight hours since Apollo had flown to
London on business. Pixie would have accompanied him
had the whole household not been in chaos getting ready
for the big party the following day. With the housekeeper,
Olympia, presenting Pixie with query after query it had
slowly dawned on her that she needed to stay on Nexos
to take charge.

'Nonsense,' Apollo had declared without hesitation.
'These matters have been managed without a wife's input
for years.'

But during that conversation Pixie had had to race
off and be horribly sick, which had driven home hard
another drawback. Hours of travel with her current delicate stomach would make her miserable and she was in
no hurry to face Apollo with the repugnant downside of
pregnancy. She was being ill an awful lot more than she
had ever expected because her morning sickness seemed
to attack at all times of the day. For that reason she had
used the party arrangements as an excuse because she
didn't want Apollo to realise just how sick she was. While
in her head she knew she should be sharing her suffer-

ing with him because he was an adult, it was a struggle to overcome her reluctance. He would fuss and she hated fuss and didn't want to be treated like an invalid. In any case they had arranged for Pixie to have her first scan that very afternoon and she planned to ask the visiting gynaecologist then about her seemingly excessive sickness.

Pixie put the phone to her ear.

'Pixie?' Holly exclaimed before bursting into a mile-a-minute speech that left Pixie, who was still drowsy, none the wiser.

'Sorry, I didn't catch all that,' she confided.

'You've seen that stupid story already, haven't you?' Holly groaned. 'Your voice sounds weird...you've been crying...'

A cold feeling slid down Pixie's spine while she leant back against the pillows, striving to overcome the nausea beginning to creep over her. It would've been easier for her to simply admit that she was pregnant and sick but her best friend would be arriving the next day for the party and she wanted to save her baby news until she saw her in person. 'What story?'

'Vito insists it's untrue...well, with that particular girl.'

'Can I phone you back, Holly?' Pixie gasped, cutting off the call and leaping from the bed in wild haste to charge for the bathroom.

Afterwards, she rested her brow down on the welcome coldness of the marble vanity counter and tried to muster the energy to clean her teeth. Oh, dear, she thought limply, it had not occurred to her that pregnancy would be quite so challenging. Certainly Holly had had a few upsets during her pregnancy but nothing similar to what Pixie was encountering.

And what had Holly been referring to? Some story in a newspaper? About Vito? No, why would she be phoning Pixie if it had been about Vito? And why would Holly think she had been *crying* about something? The chilled feeling of foreboding returned and as Pixie's brain began to function again she reached for the tablet by the bed and put Apollo's name in the search engine. The usual flock of references came up. She knew from experience that if she wanted to she could now access images of herself arriving on Nexos looking like a skinny bird in a very big sun hat that covered her face almost completely...

She sat on the edge of the bed while a tabloid page formed under the title 'Leopards don't change their spots...' And with perspiration breaking out on her clammy skin she read about how the newly married Apollo Metraxis had been pictured entering his apartment building with a very beautiful girl and emerging with her still in tow the following morning. For a few moments she thought she would be sick again but she fought the urge fiercely.

So, what she had always expected to happen *had* happened within only a few months of their wedding. It was no big deal, she told herself squarely and, casting the tablet aside, she went for a shower. Apollo had said he would try to be faithful but the very first time he had had to leave her behind he had found alternative entertainment of the sort he was most accustomed to enjoying. His behaviour sent a powerful message. Clearly, Pixie was no more important or special to him than any other woman he had slept with. How could she ever have thought otherwise?

And Izzy Jerome *was* a very beautiful girl with long corn-blonde hair and endless legs. She was also famous, a fairly recently discovered model/celebrity. Apollo's type in every way. Well, she wasn't about to make a giant scene over Izzy or do anything silly, Pixie warned herself severely. It was time to default to their original marriage setting in which they shared a business arrangement and nothing else. At least she could save face that way, she reasoned in despair, a sudden convulsive sob creeping up on her and squeezing her throat painfully tight.

But she wasn't going to cry over Apollo, Pixie told herself angrily. He wasn't worth her tears. He was selfish and shallow and his betrayal had literally been written in the stars because she had always been well aware that leopards didn't change their spots. The phone was ringing again somewhere in the distance but she ignored it, sitting on the shower seat while the water beat down on her and washed away the shameful tears. A sob escaped her straining lungs and she clenched her teeth in frustration. There was no way she was prepared to greet Apollo with red-rimmed eyes that would tell him just how badly he had hurt her.

And willpower did finally triumph over the tears. She switched off the shower and stepped out to grab a towel but only minutes later found herself throwing up again. Utterly wretched, she curled up on the cold floor for several minutes with Hector nuzzling against her legs. She petted him with a shaking hand. She felt dizzy and sick and dreadful but she wasn't about to show it. Apollo had done her a favour, she reasoned miserably. Her body was already changing. Her breasts had swelled, her waist had thickened and her tummy was no longer perfectly flat. Apollo would soon have lost interest in her anyway and it was better that it happened sooner rather than later.

After all, she had to learn to be independent again and stand on her own feet. Her baby would need her to be strong and brave. She had to cope and rise above the terrible hurt trying to overwhelm her common sense. He didn't love her; he had *never* loved her. The only woman Apollo had ever loved had been the evil stepmother who used him when he was far too young and immature to protect himself and had destroyed his trust and his ability to love. Was it any wonder that he had never had a serious relationship with a woman since then?

Slowly, clumsily, Pixie got herself upright again and began to dry her hair. Apollo would be home in a couple of hours with the gynaecologist he was flying out from London with him and she refused to humiliate herself by behaving like an emotional wreck and letting him appreciate what a fool she had been where he was concerned. Her pride would never recover from such an exposure. And how could she have fallen madly in love with a male programmed from the outset to break her heart? How stupid was that?

And even worse she had that wretched party to get through. As if that was not enough Apollo had contrived to destroy Christmas for her as well for the two of them had been invited to celebrate Christmas with Vito and Holly in Tuscany. Of course she would cry off now. She had no plans to take the shine off the festivities by attending as a betrayed and broken-hearted wife, who had nowhere else to go over Christmas. Apollo would probably take Izzy Jerome with him instead. Of course, Izzy might not still be Apollo's flavour of the month in three weeks' time, she thought wretchedly. His interest in a woman rarely lasted that long.

Squeezing herself into a stretchy skirt, Pixie blinked back fresh tears. Why was she putting on weight so fast? According to what she had read she was supposed to be gaining weight very gradually, not piling it on as though she had been eating for an entire rugby team!

In London, Apollo paced beside his private jet while he spoke to Vito. Who could ever have guessed that marriage could be so stressful? His life pre-Pixie now seemed free as the air, a time of immaturity and egotism. Back then nothing had bothered him very much, not the scandals, not the grasping women, not even the horrendous rumours and gossip about his lifestyle. He hadn't had to explain himself or defend his reputation to anyone because he truthfully hadn't cared what anyone thought about him. It hadn't mattered as long as he knew that he had done no wrong. But now he had Pixie and everything had changed out of all recognition. He had a wife who was pregnant and vulnerable and innately distrustful of him.

'The way the paparazzi follow you around it was bound to happen,' Vito contended. 'And now that you've achieved your objectives and she's pregnant...does it really matter?'

Pure rage slivered through Apollo. 'If it hurts her, it matters,' he breathed in a raw undertone. *'Of course,* it matters!'

'You don't sound quite as detached as you usually do,' his friend commented.

'Look, I'll talk to you tomorrow,' Apollo concluded, ending the call in sheer frustration.

Obviously, he wasn't detached. He was in turmoil. He was thinking things he'd never thought. He was feeling things he had never allowed himself to feel and the result was a state of mind dangerously close to panic. He boarded the jet with the fancy gynaecologist and his small team, yet another source of worry to be dealt with. Dr Floros had suggested that he call in a consultant when Pixie's blood tests had come back with an unexpectedly high count and the result had been forwarded to London. The scan would hopefully reveal whether or not there was any cause for concern. Apollo had per-

suaded the island doctor not to reveal that fact to Pixie
in advance of the scan, lest it upset her, but he knew the
older man was planning to share the result with her the
following day.

When had his life become so impossibly complicated?
An image of Pixie on their wedding day was superim-
posed over his troubled thoughts. But no, he reasoned,
it had started even before then. From the very first day
when she'd punched him Pixie had been different. She
wasn't impressed by him, she was never impressed by
him...except occasionally in bed, he conceded abstract-
edly, a shadowy smile briefly relaxing the tense line of
his sensual mouth.

Unlike other women, Pixie had only ever treated him
as an equal. She judged him by the same rules she applied to everyone else. She didn't make excuses for him
or handle him with kid gloves. She didn't believe that
his vast wealth entitled him to special treatment. In fact
she demanded more from him than any woman had ever
demanded, only her currency of choice wasn't cash or
gifts. Apollo had learnt the hard way that cash or gifts
were easy to give while everything else was a challenge
demanding more than he was usually prepared to give.

During the flight random memories drifted through
his mind. Pixie, grinning with triumph and punching
the air after that insane dive she had made from the top
deck of *Circe*. Pixie staring dreamily out to sea as the
sun went down in splendour, saying, 'You really don't
appreciate how lucky you are to see this every day.' Pixie
wandering round the picturesque narrow village streets
on Nexos, admiring colourful flowerboxes, sleeping cats,
starlit eyes wide with interest while she drank lemon-
ade in the café overlooking the harbour and watched the
fishermen bringing in their catch. She made everything

fresh, Apollo acknowledged in growing bewilderment; she made him see things through less jaded eyes.

Pixie could feel her facial muscles lock as she descended the stairs to welcome the arrivals. She refused to look at Apollo but she was seethingly conscious of him standing back in a stylishly crumpled beige linen suit teamed with a white tee shirt. She showed the doctor, the technician and the nurse into the room where their equipment could be set up and Olympia brought a tray of tea and snacks out to the terrace for them.

'Pixie...' Apollo said then, having demonstrated unusual patience for such an impatient man. 'Could I have a word?'

No, no way, she wanted to scream at him but she couldn't let herself scream. There would be no discussion about Izzy Jerome or about the promise he had given about *trying* to stay faithful. What was done was done and there was really nothing more to say. All she had to do now was draw a line under their marriage as such and default to the useful guidelines printed in her prenuptial contract.

'Your office,' she suggested, stealing an involuntary glance at him.

He hadn't shaved and he was still gorgeous. Dark stubble shadowed his strong jaw line and outlined his superbly kissable lips. His black hair was messy, his stunning green eyes glittering warily below his black velvet lashes. He was sexy as sin and a pang of wanton lust pierced her pelvis. Guilty colour washed her pallor away. He had cheated on her with a blonde beauty, so how could she still respond to him on a physical level? Self-loathing inflamed her while she picked her passage through the team of caterers fussing over the chairs that were being carried into the ballroom where the party would be held.

The mere prospect of the party made her grit her teeth. All those people would be attending primarily to see her in her role as the wife of Apollo Metraxis, people who would know he was already playing away with another woman, and yet Pixie would have to pretend that nothing was wrong because that was what she had agreed to do when she chose to marry him. Luckily pretending, however, would allow her to retain a certain dignity, she reminded herself doggedly.

Her visceral reaction was to scream, shout and claw at Apollo and from the curious glances he was angling at her she could see that a major scene was what he expected. But Pixie was determined not to lower herself to that level. Whatever else he was, Apollo was the father of her child and, whether she liked it or not, he would remain a feature of her life for many years in the future. She was determined not to embarrass herself in front of him by revealing that she had made the mistake of becoming emotionally involved.

'I'm relieved that you're giving us the chance to talk before Mr Rollins gives you the scan,' Apollo murmured in an unusually quiet voice.

Was he ashamed? No, Apollo didn't do shame or fidelity when it came to sex, she reasoned painfully. He was probably genuinely grateful that she wasn't making a big scene.

Pixie stationed herself by the window that looked across the sloping gardens and over the top of the trees and out to sea. She steeled her spine. 'I want us to separate—'

'No,' Apollo interrupted immediately.

'It's in the pre-nup agreement,' Pixie reminded him. 'Once I'm pregnant I can if I wish ask to live separately

and I would like to return to the UK as soon as it can
be arranged.'

Apollo was powerfully knocked off balance by that
announcement. Yes, that was in the agreement because
before he married her he had assumed that he would want
his freedom back as soon as possible. Had ever a man
been so bloody stupid and blind? he railed at himself in
furious frustration. 'That is exactly what I *don't* want.'

Pixie rested icy grey eyes on his lean bronzed face. 'I
don't care what you want.'

'You're not even giving me a chance to explain?'

'No, that kind of discussion would challenge my ability to be civil to you,' Pixie admitted hoarsely, because
inside herself where it didn't show she was breaking
apart. She hated him and yet she still wanted to be near
him. She loathed him for betraying her and yet her weak,
wanton body still hummed in direct response to the in-
sanely hot attraction he exuded. The very thought of not
seeing Apollo again for months on end threatened to rip
her into tiny pieces but she knew the difference between
right and wrong and she knew what she had to do to restore the boundaries she needed to feel safe.

And she could never *ever* feel safe with an unfaithful man. It didn't matter that it had only happened once,
what mattered was that she had made the mistake of
thinking of their marriage as a real marriage and now
she was being destroyed because she loved him. But he
hadn't asked her for her love or her possessiveness and
he had even warned her that fidelity would be a struggle
for him. How far in those circumstances could she blame
him for what he had done? She had fallen for him and
that was her mistake, not his.

'This is crazy...' Apollo breathed with sudden raw-ness, big brown hands settling over her slight shoulders. 'You won't even look at me!'

'I'm being polite.'

'That isn't you... I don't *know* you like this!' Apollo growled in frustration. 'Shout at me, kick me...whatever!'

'Why would I do that?' Pixie forced a frozen little smile to her lips. 'We've enjoyed a successful business arrangement. My brother is safe and learning how to live without gambling and I'm carrying a baby I want very much. Now you can return to the freewheeling life you prefer.'

Even though his temper was cruelly challenged by that speech, his big hands withdrew from her tense shoulders and dropped away to slowly ball into fists by his sides because he genuinely didn't want to argue with her and upset her. 'Mr Rollins should be ready for you now,' he pronounced with savage quietness.

Pixie chewed at her full lower lip, blaming him for the fact that the scan she had been eager to have had now been horribly overshadowed by his betrayal and her heartbreak. But maybe seeing the shape of her baby on a screen would restore her and cure the agony clawing up inside her. It hurt so much not to have Apollo any more. It hurt not to be able to allow herself to touch him. But a kick, never mind a kiss, would have released the pent-up rage and hurt she was holding back.

She wanted to tell him that she had gone down to the animal rehabilitation centre on the outskirts of the village while he was away and had met the staff and occupants as well as spotting a little dog very similar to Hector. She had wanted to share that with Apollo but then she wanted to share *everything* with Apollo, had in fact got used to treating him like her best friend, and in the wake of his infidelity that was a really terrifying revelation. What had happened to her pride? But now she could feel the new distance forming inside her and she clung to that barrier in desperation.

Having set up the equipment, the nurse and the technician were ready to give Pixie her scan. She got up on the mobile examination table, rested her head back on the pillow and pushed down her skirt to expose her tummy while the consultant talked smoothly about what she could expect to see. He referred to her blood test, which surprised her. Clearly he had consulted the island doctor for that result and she wondered why.

The gel the technician put on her stomach was cool and she shivered, eyes flying wide when Apollo moved forward and closed a hand over her knotted fingers. The amazing racing sound of the baby's heartbeat filled the silence and she smiled in sheer wonder. The wand moved and then the heartbeat surged again.

'Two babies, Mrs Metraxis.'

'Two?' she echoed in astonishment.

'Twins. I suspected a multiple pregnancy when I saw the results of your first blood test...'

Shocked, Pixie locked her eyes to the screen while the consultant outlined the shadowy forms of her children. Children, not one child as she had simply assumed. It was an enormous change to get her head around. She wondered if that explained the heavy nausea she was enduring and the physical changes that were already altering her body.

Apollo studied the screen in horror. Two of them? Two babies struggling to make space in Pixie's tiny body? How could that be? That had to make everything more dangerous.

Pixie yanked her hand from Apollo's because he was crushing her fingers. She glanced up at him, reading the raw tension etched in his hard features. He wasn't pleased. But then why would he be? He had only needed one child and two would presumably be more hassle and expense. The nurse wiped off the gel and helped her back to her feet. She took a seat for yet another blood test and shut her eyes tight sooner than see the needle while Apollo took up position behind her and rested his hands down heavily on her shoulders.

She told the consultant about her frequent nausea. He explained that that could occur in a twin pregnancy and that it should settle down by the end of her first trimester, but that if it began to impact on her health she would need support. He mentioned that the twins each had their own placenta, which lessened the chance of complications. The information he gave her was very practical and Pixie was happy to thank him and leave while Apollo demonstrated a dismaying eagerness to stay behind and talk to the medical team.

Apollo's blood had run cold throughout his entire body when the word 'complications' struck him like blow. He felt sick. Mr Rollins informed him unasked that sex was still perfectly fine. Ironically, Apollo had never felt less horny and he was suddenly feeling very guilty. If anything went wrong it would be his fault. He had planned this pregnancy, done everything possible to make it happen and now that he had he was discovering that he had hitched a ride on a rocket that he could no longer control. Not since his troubled childhood had he been made to feel so helpless. By the time the medical team departed on the helicopter to head back to the airport, Apollo was in a seriously sombre mood.

Pixie settled down happily with a pot of tea on the shaded terrace with Hector at her feet. Two babies, my goodness, weren't they going to be a handful? She was in shock but, after hearing her babies' heartbeats, she was excited and pleased as well. She sipped her tea and wondered if the twins would be identical or non-identical and whether they would be boys or girls or even one of each. It was a huge relief to have something other than Apollo to think about.

Apollo strode out onto the terrace and surveyed her. 'I can't let you leave me,' he intoned grimly. 'I *have* to be part of this. They are my children too. I need to be sure you're healthy and looking after yourself.'

'What about what I need?' Pixie countered, eyes narrowing as she looked back at him because he was standing in sunlight, tall and bronzed and muscular as a god in stature and so beautiful he didn't seem quite real to her.

'You need my support.'

'No, I don't. I've been independent all my life,' Pixie traded without hesitation.

Apollo leant back against the low wall separating the terrace from the garden and tossed a squeaky toy at Hector, who bounded after it with glee. 'I don't want you to be independent.'

'Tough. We made a business arrangement,' Pixie reminded him. 'Getting pregnant is my get-out-of-jail-free card and I'm playing it.'

'You're being unreasonable.'

'I love the island. I like my life here but this is *your* house, *your* island and I don't want to live in your house on your island,' Pixie explained without apology.

Apollo breathed in slow and deep and practised a patience that he was in no way accustomed to practising. 'We'll discuss it after the party tomorrow.'

Her life had fallen apart, Pixie thought, suddenly losing the high of finding out that she was carrying two babies. She was about to become a single mum, which most poignantly was something she had once sworn she would never be. But that was life, she told herself, knocking you back on your heels and changing things without warning. And she would be a liar if she argued that she couldn't have foreseen the breakdown of their marriage. After all, that breakdown had been foreseen in the pre-nuptial agreement she had signed and all the conditions for that breakdown laid out in advance. She had read the terms and she had even read the small print. She knew that she had rights and that Apollo couldn't ignore them.

Apollo crossed the tiles towards her and studied her with gorgeous glittering green eyes. 'I don't want this marriage to end. I don't want a divorce,' he declared. 'I don't want you to leave Nexos either.'

After a noisy pummelling session with his squeaky toy, Hector sneaked across the floor and hovered uneasily near Apollo's feet before he gingerly dropped the toy there. Muttering something shaken in Greek, Apollo stilled and then he bent, scooped it up and threw it and Hector went careening after it. 'He brought the toy to me. He *finally* brought it to me!' he exclaimed in amazement.

'I never said my dog had good taste,' Pixie remarked, in no mood to be captivated.

The following morning, the day of the party, Pixie was following her usual routine of being horrendously sick when Apollo joined her in the bathroom. 'Go away!' she shrieked furiously.

'No, this is my business,' Apollo declared, crouching down to loop her hair out of the way and support her.

'I *hate* you!' Pixie snapped with pure venom because it was the last straw that he should witness her in such a state when all her defences were down, and there were many more such tart exchanges before her stomach settled again.

Having cleaned her up with unblemished cool, Apollo carried her back to bed. 'Do you want me to cancel the party?'

'You can't. Half our guests are already on their way,' she groaned. 'I'll be fine once Holly gets here.'

'I haven't had sex with anyone but you since we got married,' Apollo announced just when she was least expecting any reference to that burning issue.

'Don't believe you,' Pixie gasped, turning over on her side to avoid looking at him. 'Nobody would believe you. I'm not stupid. It's what you do, it's who you are...you probably can't even help it.'

'It's not who I am!' Apollo bit out hotly from between clenched white teeth, his eyes emerald bright and accusing. 'The least you can do is give me the chance to explain.'

Pixie closed her eyes tight and played dead. His sudden anger had unnerved her. She didn't fear him but right then she didn't feel equal to the challenge of such an emotive confrontation. In fact suddenly all she wanted was Holly's reassuringly soothing presence. Tears stung her eyes behind the lowered lids.

'Izzy is Jeremy Slater's kid sister. Vito and I went to school with Jeremy. Although you haven't met him yet, he's a close friend. Izzy was at a dinner I attended. I've met her before and she asked me for a lift because she was visiting someone with an apartment in the same building as my London penthouse. I thought nothing of it,' Apollo admitted grittily. 'I wasn't particularly surprised either when the paparazzi jumped out to photograph us when we arrived because Izzy's every move is currently prime fodder for the tabloid newspapers.'

'So, according to you, you simply gave her a lift,' Pixie recited. 'How does that explain her still being with you the next morning?'

'She spent the night with whoever she was visiting. She phoned me first thing and asked me if I could drop her off on my way into the office. She was waiting for me in the lobby and we left the building together.'

'When you were caught on camera again. Why didn't your bodyguards intervene?'

'Because I suspected that Izzy was using me to raise her own profile and, not having thought through the situation, I saw no harm in it and waved them back,' Apollo ground out angrily.

His explanation covered the facts but his generosity towards Izzy Jerome's craving for publicity when he himself loathed paparazzi attention infuriated her. Since when had Apollo not 'thought through' a situation? He must've realised how the press would present those photos, one taken the night before, the next early the next morning.

'I'm sorry,' she pronounced flatly. 'I don't believe you.'

The door thudded closed on his exit and only then did her tension ease a little yet she had never felt so empty. She had not realised that she could love anyone as much as she loved Apollo and she had not realised that losing someone could hurt so much that it hurt to breathe. And it was a lesson she truly wished she had not had to learn. She had lain awake a long time the night before. Apollo had presumably slept in another room and ironically his absence had distressed her as much as his presence would have done. It was as though she were being ripped slowly apart, divided between wanting him and not wanting him.

Vito and Holly arrived mid-afternoon. As soon as

Pixie heard Holly's bright voice echoing up from the hall she called down to her friend from the upper landing. Apollo and Vito looked up. Pixie reddened and waved to excuse herself for not having gone downstairs to welcome their guests.

'I'm pregnant,' she told Holly baldly. 'And, yes, it was planned.'

'Is that why Apollo is looking a little ragged round the edges?'

'No... I think that was caused by the doctor telling us that we're having twins.'

'Twins?' Holly squealed in excitement. 'When are you due?'

As the friends shared due dates, because Holly was expecting her second child, they went downstairs by a service staircase and settled down with cool drinks in the orangery with its tall shady plants and softly playing indoor fountain.

'Vito told me about the will and that you were planning to have a child with Apollo,' Holly confided then.

Pixie sighed heavily.

'And you broke the rules, didn't you?' Holly whispered, anxiously searching Pixie's tense little face and shadowed eyes. 'You went and fell madly in love with his fancy-ass yacht.'

Pixie didn't trust herself to laugh or speak and she jerked her chin down in confirmation.

Holly groaned out loud.

'I wanted a child and because I wasn't very good at... er...dating I thought that Apollo could be my best chance of ever having one,' Pixie admitted very quietly. 'I should tell you now...we are separating after the party.'

'Is it really that cut and dried? I mean, even Vito, who generally assumes the worst of Apollo when women are involved, thinks that there's no way that Apollo would have slept with Izzy Jerome. She's Jeremy's kid sister and sisters are off-limits between friends. And Apollo has *un*invited Izzy from your party,' Holly completed with satisfaction.

'Izzy Jerome was on the guest list?' Pixie gasped in dismay.

'She's not any more,' Holly emphasised. 'I don't think he is involved with her. She's very young, you know, still a teenager.'

'It doesn't matter.' Pixie lifted her head high and sipped at her drink. 'The best way forward for us now is for us to go our separate ways. That was planned from the start.'

Holly shook her head. 'I can't believe you signed up for that. I thought you hated him.'

Pixie said nothing because there was a sour taste in her mouth. Only days had passed since she had planned to tell her friend how very different Apollo was from his public image but recent events had proved her wrong in all her assumptions. In truth she supposed that she had stupidly idealised Apollo to justify the reality that she had fallen in love with him.

'Let me see what you're wearing tonight,' Holly urged in a welcome change of subject.

Pixie took her up to the bedroom to show her the long scarlet dress in its garment bag. 'Apollo had it designed and I don't like it much…it's a wee bit slutty, don't you think? I have no idea what he's wearing.'

Holly skimmed a thoughtful fingertip over the black corset lacing round the bust line. 'Gangster's moll?'

'Well, at least there's no fairy wings included,' Pixie commented flatly. 'But there is a very ornate piece of valuable jewellery which he brought back from London and he evidently expects me to wear it with the costume.'

Pixie opened the worn leather box on the dressing table and listened to Holly ooh and ah over the fabulously flamboyant ruby necklace and drop earrings. She turned her head and glanced back at the red dress again. There was something about it, something eerily familiar but she couldn't pin down what it was.

Dressing for dinner, she donned the costume. She decided it was fortunate that pregnancy had swelled her boobs because the gathered, dipping neckline positively demanded a glimpse of bosom. She tightened the laces, noting with wry appreciation that she finally had the chest she had long dreamt of having. But like her marriage to Apollo, it was an illusion, she thought morosely, for when she had finally delivered her twins she would probably return to being pretty much flat-chested again.

Apollo strode in and she stopped dead to stare at him. He was tricked out like a pirate in tall black boots and fitted breeches with a white ruffled shirt and a sword. And being Apollo and fantastically handsome, he looked spectacular and electrifyingly sexy.

'I gather that I'm a pirate's lady,' Pixie guessed.

'A pirate's treasure,' Apollo quipped. 'You're not wearing the rubies.'

He extracted the necklace from the box and handed her the earrings. 'This set belonged to my mother. It hasn't been worn since she died. I had it cleaned and reset for you in London.'

The eye-catching rubies settled coolly against her skin and she slowly attached the earrings, watching them gleam with inner fire as they swung in the lamp light. 'Thanks,' she said stiltedly.

A very large dinner party awaited them on the ground

floor. With surprising formality Apollo brought his relatives forward one by one to meet Pixie. There were innumerable aunties and uncles and cousins. She marvelled at his calm control under stress and his polished manners. He was essentially behaving like a proud new husband. Nobody could ever have guessed that that dream was already dead and buried. It had been a dream, she reminded herself doggedly, a dream that could never have become reality with Apollo Metraxis in a leading role.

In the ballroom she watched Apollo socialising and frowned. It wasn't fair that she could barely drag her eyes off his tall, powerful physique; it wasn't right or decent that she still felt his magnetic pull. And Apollo dressed up like a pirate was pure perfect fantasy. The arrogant tilt of his dark head, the breadth of his shoulders, his narrow waist and lean, tight hips, the long muscular line of his thighs in skin-tight pants. Her mouth ran dry watching him and her weakness filled her with self-loathing.

Apollo, meanwhile, was in a filthy mood. The planning had gone perfectly but the timing had gone seriously askew. He should have known better; he should have known not to waste his time trying to be something he was not. Since when had he been romantic? What did he even *know* about being romantic? And in any case, she hadn't even *noticed*, which said all that needed to be said. He had taken the cover of her battered romantic paperback and had the outfits copied. Even the costume designer had gazed at him as though he were crazy and he felt like an idiot for going for the pirate theme. Even so, he wasn't going down without a fight.

'I'm no good at slow dances,' Pixie protested when Apollo slowly raised her out of her seat and took her away from Holly, whom she had clung to throughout the evening.

'So, stand on my feet,' Apollo advised, wrapping her slender body into his arms with the kind of strength she couldn't fight without making a scene.

Murderously conscious that their guests were watching them, Pixie pressed her face against his chest and breathed in deep. He smelled so good she wanted to bottle him. Her fingers spread across his powerful shoulders and she drifted in a world of inner pain, wavering wildly between hating and craving and loving. She had missed him so much when he was away from her in London and now she had a whole future of missing him ahead of her.

'I won't agree to a separation,' Apollo breathed softly above her head.

'I don't need your agreement. I'll just leave.'

He went rigid in her arms and missed a step. Pixie was fighting back tears, reminding herself that they were in the middle of a party, that they were the centre of attention as much because she was a new bride as because the bridegroom had been outed as a cheat little more than forty-eight hours previously.

'I'll buy you a house in London...but you stay safe *here* until I have that organised for you.'

'I don't need your help.'

'I'll call you when I've set up the house and you can fly out and give me your opinion.'

Pixie swallowed back a sudden inexplicable sob because, without warning, Apollo had stopped fighting her and had backed off. Instead of feeling relieved, she felt more lost and alone than ever. They really were splitting up. Their marriage was over.

The three weeks that followed were a walking blur for Pixie. Apollo had left Nexos as soon as the last of their guests had departed. He had not attempted to have another serious conversation with her. Those last words exchanged on the dance floor, with her ridiculous threat to just walk out, lingered with her. Yes, she could walk out, she conceded, but she couldn't just walk away from her feelings, the painful feelings that accompanied her everywhere no matter where she was or what she was doing. She couldn't stop thinking about Apollo or fighting off the suspicion that she had condemned him on the basis of his reputation rather than on the evidence.

So preoccupied was she that she barely noticed that her bouts of sickness were fading away. She had to move into maternity clothes rather sooner than she had hoped because most of her fashionable outfits were too fitted to cope with her swollen breasts and vanishing waistline. She purchased new clothes online, loose-cut separates picked for comfort rather than elegance. With Apollo absent she discovered that she didn't care what she looked like. He phoned every week to civilly enquire after her health, and when he asked her if she could join him in London on a certain date her heart sank, because once he showed her the house he expected her to occupy she assumed that the dust would settle on their official separation. Evidently he had accepted that their relationship, their intimacy, was over now.

And wasn't that what she had wanted? How could she move forward without putting their marriage behind her? Apollo had denied infidelity but he hadn't put up much of a fight against her disbelief, had he? But like a sneaky snake in the grass in the back of her mind lurked the dangerous thought that she could, if she wanted, offer him a second chance. She was so ashamed of that indefensible thought that it woke her up at night in a cold sweat. She understood that her brain was struggling to find a solution to her unending grief and sense of deep loss and she knew that the forgiving approach worked for some couples but she knew it would never work for her. Nor would it work for a male like Apollo, who needed strong boundaries and punishing consequences because he wouldn't respect anything else.

Pixie arrived back in London late afternoon in late December with Hector in tow. A limo met her at the airport and whisked her back to the penthouse apartment. Apollo was flying in from LA and had told her that he would not be arriving until shortly before their scheduled meeting. That was why it was a surprise for Pixie to be curled up on a sofa with her dog in front of the television and suddenly be told by Manfred that she had visitors. As she stood up Hector bolted for cover under a chair.

A tall man with prematurely greying dark hair walked in with an oddly self-conscious air but Pixie's attention leapt straight off him towards the highly recognisable youthful blonde accompanying him.

'I'm Jeremy Slater and I apologise for walking in on you like this but my sister has something she has to say to you,' the man told her stiffly. 'Izzy...you have the floor...'

The tall, slender blonde fixed strained blue eyes on Pixie and burst into immediate speech. 'I'm really sorry for what I did. I set Apollo up as cover. I knew he was married but I didn't think about that. I'm afraid I was only thinking about what suited me.'

Pixie was frowning in bewilderment. *'You set Apollo up?'* she repeated blankly.

'I knew that if I was spotted with Apollo, the paps would assume that we were together and that they wouldn't look any more closely into who I was staying with in that building,' she spelled out tautly.

'What my sister *isn't* saying,' Jeremy interposed drily, 'is that she has been involved with a famous actor, who keeps an apartment in Apollo's building. As that man is married, both my sister and he wished to keep their relationship out of the public eye.'

'I didn't intend to cause anyone any trouble,' Izzy said pleadingly.

'But you weren't too concerned when you did cause that trouble,' Pixie pointed out, her stomach churning with shock. 'I can see that I have your brother to thank for this explanation being made.'

'I couldn't stand back and let Apollo take the fall for something he didn't do,' Jeremy declared cheerfully. 'He's been guilty as charged so often and I'm certain that that means that he suffers in the credibility stakes.'

'Yes,' Pixie agreed, her face hot with shame because even she hadn't really listened to Apollo when he'd said he was innocent.

She hadn't asked the relevant questions and she hadn't asked if he could prove his story. In fact she hadn't given him a fair hearing in any way and in retrospect that acknowledgement humbled her. In common with any other bystander she had indeed assumed that he was guilty as charged, but she had had much less excuse than other people because she had lived with Apollo for months and knew that he was something more, something deeper than the heartless womaniser he appeared to be in public.

Jeremy and Izzy departed soon afterwards with Jeremy remarking that he hoped they would soon meet in more sociable circumstances. His sister, however, said nothing, probably guessing that Pixie never wanted to see her again if she could help it.

After that visit, Pixie went to bed but of course she couldn't sleep. She had never trusted Apollo and had essentially regarded her distrust as a trait that strengthened her. Only now was she seeing the downside of that outlook. Looking for the worst and always expecting the worst from a man was not a healthy approach and it was unfair. Even worse, using distrust as a first line of defence had crucially blinded her to what was actually happening in their marriage. She should have recognised how far Apollo had already drifted from his original blueprint for a marriage that was a business arrangement. Time after time he had done things, *said* things that defied that blueprint and she had ignored that reality. After all, *she* had changed—why shouldn't he have changed too?

The next morning it was a struggle for Pixie to eat any breakfast. She had forced a separation on Apollo and had voluntarily given him back his freedom. She had well and truly proved to be her own worst enemy. Pride and distrust had driven her into rejecting the man she loved. Could he forgive her for that? Could he forgive her for misjudging him?

Would her misjudgement and their marriage even matter to him now? After all, his inheritance would soon be fully his because by the time their children were born he would have met the exact terms of his father's will. Nowhere in that will did it state that Apollo had to be still living with his wife.

A limousine collected her at half past nine, wafting her through streets soon to be thronged with Christmas shoppers. Shop windows were bright with decorations and sparkle. Pixie had dressed with care and not in one of her less than flattering maternity outfits. She had put on a green dress. True it was a little tight over her bust but it gave her a shape and her legs were the same as they had always been. In truth, she reflected unhappily as the car drew up outside a smart city town house in a tree-lined Georgian square with a private park, she would never be able to hold a candle to the likes of Izzy Jerome in looks. On board *Circe*, she had marvelled at Apollo's insatiable hunger for her and revelled in it. Now, she had to ask herself if she had anything more substantial to offer a male of his sophistication...

Apollo opened the door of the house himself, which shook her because he almost always had staff around to take care of such tasks.

Pixie stepped over the threshold. She glanced up at him, encountering shimmering green eyes below lashes as rich and dark as black lace, and her heartbeat raced, butterflies unleashed to fly free in her stomach. 'Apollo...' she acknowledged jerkily.

She came to a halt to stare in wide-eyed amazement at the lavish Christmas tree in the hall and the glorious trails of holly festooning the hall fireplace and the stairs. 'Oh, my goodness, this house...it's all decorated for Christmas,' she muttered inanely. 'And it's still furnished.'

'Relax. The furniture and the decorations are mine. This house was rented out for years. My father owned it but he didn't use it and it was too large for me to use while I was still single,' Apollo told her, gently but firmly urging her down into the armchair set by the small crackling fire in the hearth. 'Sit down and stop stressing.'

Pixie sat but she couldn't stop stressing. Apollo was exquisitely well-dressed in a formal navy suit, cuff links glinting at the cuffs of a fine white shirt, and she remembered him dressed like a pirate and every skin cell leapt up in sensual recollection. 'You want me to live in your father's house? I thought I was supposed to live in a house you bought me?'

Apollo dealt her an impassive appraisal that told her nothing about his mood. 'I understand that Jeremy called on you with Izzy last night,' he remarked stiffly.

Pixie flinched and paled, unnerved by that reminder. Of course, it had been foolish of her not to appreciate that his friend would naturally have told him about that visit. 'Yes, I'm so, so sorry. I misjudged you and refused to listen and there's no excuse for that, is there?'

'Perhaps there is,' Apollo conceded, sharply disconcerting her with that measured response. 'Maybe if I'd said more sooner, you *would* have wanted to listen to what I had to say.'

Sick with nerves, Pixie curled her hands tightly together. 'I'm really sorry,' she said shakily again. 'I didn't give you a chance.'

'I have a bad reputation with women,' Apollo allowed reflectively. 'But in one sense it's unjustified. I have always ended one relationship before I embark on another. I don't do crossovers or betrayals. That's a small point but that's how I live. I don't cheat on anyone.'

Her nails dug into her palms because she was so very tense and afraid of saying the wrong thing. She had said she was sorry but she didn't want to keep on saying sorry and she didn't want to crawl either. 'I understand.'

'We were talking about this house,' Apollo reminded her, lounging elegantly back against the marble console table behind him.

'Y-yes,' she stammered.

'I want you to live here with me. With twins on the horizon we definitely need a spacious family house.'

Her smooth brow indented as she struggled to understand. 'Are you saying that you can forgive me for the way I behaved on Nexos?'

'There are still things that you have to forgive me for,' Apollo told her tautly. 'When we first married I pretended that I was still holding your brother's debt over you because I saw that debt as a guarantee that you would do as you were told.'

Her smooth brow furrowed. 'You pretended? In what way?'

'I paid off the debt in its entirety before our marriage. I didn't want any further dealings with the thug your brother owed that money to,' he admitted.

Pixie nodded understanding. 'The carrot and the stick approach again...right? Well, you're good at faking.'

'Thank you,' Apollo murmured wryly. 'I should've been more honest with you though.'

'We both hugged our secrets back then. It takes time to learn to trust someone.'

'You're the first woman I've ever trusted,' Apollo admitted. 'You know the worst of me. You've seen the bad stuff. Give me a chance to show you the good things I can do.'

Pixie unfroze and stared up at him. 'You *are* willing to forgive me for misjudging you,' she suddenly appreciated in wonderment.

His smile slanted into a heart-stopping grin. 'As I can't live without you I don't think I have much choice about that.'

'You can't live,' she began incredulously, '*without* me?'

'I've got remarkably used to having you and Hector around,' Apollo told her almost flippantly.

'H-have you?' Pixie mumbled uncertainly.

'Even though trying to plant an idea in your head is sometimes like drilling through concrete.'

'What idea were you trying to plant?'

'That we could be happy together and stay together and married for ever.'

'You don't do for ever,' Pixie argued, her voice taking on a shrill edge of disbelief.

'But then I met you and ever since then everything I *thought* I knew has been proven wrong,' Apollo admitted gravely. 'That unnerved me...but there it is. You've turned my life upside down and, strangest of all, I've discovered that I *like* it this way.'

Pixie's mouth had run dry. 'I'm not sure I understand.'

Apollo reached down a lean brown hand towards hers and in a sudden movement she grasped it. He tugged her upright. 'I want to show you something and ask you a special question.'

Blinking rapidly, her heart hammering inside her chest, Pixie let him urge her upstairs. He pushed open the door on a bedroom but her attention leapt straight to the garment hanging in front of a wardrobe. 'What's that?' she gasped, for it looked remarkably like a white wedding dress.

Apollo dropped fluidly down on one knee while she stared at him as if he had lost his wits, her grey eyes huge and questioning. 'Pixie...will you marry me?'

'Wh-what?' she stuttered shakily.

'I'm trying to do it right this time. I love you,' Apollo breathed huskily. 'Will you marry me?'

'But we're already married,' she whispered in a small voice. 'You...*love*...me?'

'Much more than I ever thought I could love anyone.'

And the power in Pixie's legs just went and she dropped down on her knees in front of him. 'You mean it...you're not just saying it?'

Apollo flipped open the small jewellery box in his hand and extracted a ruby ring. 'And this is the ruby ring I intended to give you before the fancy dress party but sadly it would have been the wrong time.'

Pixie watched in reverence as he eased the glorious

ring onto her wedding finger. 'Is this an engagement ring?' she whispered.

With an impatient groan, Apollo leapt back upright and bent to scoop Pixie up and plant her at the foot of the bed. 'Yes, it is, and we need to start moving quickly. That is if you're willing to stay married to me?'

'Yes, I am... I'm kind of...' Pixie hesitated and then lifted her bemused head high to look up at him '...attached to you, *so* attached I can't bear having you out of my sight and the last few weeks have been sheer *hell*,' she admitted feelingly. 'I don't know when it happened because I started out convinced I hated you and somewhere along the way I fell madly in love with you.'

Sheer relief rippled through Apollo's lean, powerful frame. '*Thee mou*...you made me wait for that, you little witch. Would you like me to help you put on your wedding gown?'

Another wave of bewilderment rocked Pixie. 'Why would I put on a wedding gown?'

'Because your very romantic husband wants to take you to a church to renew our vows...and this time, we'll mean *every* word and every promise, *koukla mou*. I wanted to see you in a white dress.'

Pixie felt as though her brain had gone on holiday. She was poleaxed by that information.

Apollo lifted her off the bed and unzipped her dress, pushing it off her shoulders until it slid down her arms and dropped to the rug. 'I like the lingerie,' he growled soft and low.

'We're going to renew our vows? You've actually arranged that?' she exclaimed as her brain absorbed that incredible concept. 'Oh, I like that. I *like* that idea very much...'

'And then we're going to fly out to Tuscany to spend Christmas with Vito and Holly.'

All of a sudden, Pixie became a ball of energy. She whirled away from him, a slender vision in white lace underpinnings, and yanked the wedding dress off the wardrobe at speed. 'I hope it fits.'

'I told the designer you were pregnant and she made allowances.'

Pixie wrenched off the bag and dived into the wedding gown as if her life depended on it and indeed at that moment it felt as if her life did depend on it. Apollo was making all her dreams come true at once. He was trying to rewrite their history and she adored him for that piece of unashamed sentimentality. He was, after all, offering her the white wedding dress and the church she had once dreamt of. He loved her. Could she truly believe that? The ruby sparkled enticingly on her finger and she heaved a happy sigh. When Apollo began organising church blessings and getting down on bended knee to propose, it was time to take him very seriously indeed, she thought happily.

It was an exquisitely delicate and elegant lace dress and Apollo was fantastic at doing up hooks. Dainty pearlised shoes completed the ensemble and she dug her feet into them with a sigh. 'You've thought of everything.'

'I had to organise it all in advance even though I was scared you would say no. My first romantic scenario fell very flat,' Apollo pointed out in his own defence. 'Your bouquet is downstairs.'

'What *first* romantic scenario?' she prompted with a frown.

'The one where I had the cover of your bodice-ripping paperback copied for our fancy dress costumes,' Apollo extended. 'The one where I dressed up as a stupid pirate and you were *supposed* to recognise the outfits from the book cover.'

Pixie gasped and her grey eyes widened to their fullest extent. She recalled that sense of familiarity when she had seen the red dress he had had designed for her and she grinned. 'It was the first romance I ever read. I bought it at a church jumble sale...but when I got older, I didn't think it was realistic to believe I could ever meet a man as swoonworthy as the hero...and here you are, Apollo Metraxis, and you're hotter than the fires of hell!'

'Even so, you didn't notice,' he reminded her doggedly.

'I definitely noticed how sexy you looked,' she confided, her cheeks turning pink, and her heart literally sang at the image of Apollo going to so much trouble in an effort to be romantic and please her. 'Breeches and knee boots are a great look on you, so maybe you'll put that on again for me some day and I faithfully promise to demonstrate my appreciation. That night, I'm afraid I was too locked into the hurt of the Izzy business to notice. I'm sorry.'

'And I'm sorry you were hurt,' Apollo confided tenderly as he urged her back down the stairs, grabbed the bridal bouquet out of another room and planted it into her hands. 'Let's get to the church, Mrs Metraxis...'

And the little ceremony was glorious and everything Pixie could have dreamt of it being. She could see the love in Apollo's brilliant green eyes and when he actually paused afterwards on the church steps and posed with his arm round her for the paparazzi, he smiled with even greater brilliance and a level of happiness he had never known before.

'What time are Vito and Holly expecting us?' Pixie whispered as they climbed into the waiting car.

'My social secretary rang them to let them know we

wouldn't be arriving until later,' Apollo revealed. 'I don't want to share you just yet. I want a few hours to privately appreciate my very beautiful, pregnant-with-twins wife.'

'And how do you feel about the babies?'

'Over the moon now that we'll be in London with the best possible medical care on the doorstep,' Apollo told her, drawing her close, the heat of his big frame sending a little pulse of fiery awareness through her. 'I was worrying far too much and your consultant reassured me. You'll be in the best possible hands for the duration of your pregnancy.'

'*Your* hands,' Pixie muttered, pressing his palm against her cheek in a loving gesture. 'You'll look after me... I know you will.'

'You're my whole world and our children are part of us both. I can't believe I ever thought I'd be able to walk away and take a back seat in their lives.'

'Well, you won't be walking away any place now,' Pixie said cheerfully, resting shining eyes on him. 'I love you, Apollo, and there's no escape.'

'And you're the love I didn't believe existed as well as the most amazing woman I've ever met,' he growled, claiming her parted lips with his in a long, deep, hungry kiss of possession that thrilled her right down to her toes. 'Where else will I find a woman insane enough to dive off the top of my yacht? And expect me to be pleased? Or threaten me with a miniature Arab Prince as a rival?'

EPILOGUE

AT SIXTEEN MONTHS OLD, Sofia Metraxis was a force to be reckoned with. She ran over to her brother, Tobias, swiped his toy truck off him and sat back to bat away his attempts to retrieve it.

'That wasn't nice,' Pixie said, scooping up Tobias, who was crying over the loss of his favourite toy.

'You don't do nice, do you, Alpha baby?' Apollo chuckled, lifting his daughter and exchanging the truck for another toy to return it to Tobias.

'She's just cheeky,' Pixie contended.

'And bossy...wonder where she gets that from,' Apollo teased, watching Tobias stop crying to play with his truck. 'I can't get over how different they are.'

And the twins were. Tobias was the quieter twin, clever and thoughtful and methodical even in play. Sofia was all bells and whistles and complaints and needed rather less sleep. Together the two children had transformed their parents' lives, ensuring that Apollo and Pixie spent more time enjoying the wide open spaces and beaches available on Nexos than in their comfortable London town house.

Pixie had spent all of her pregnancy in London. Only after the birth of the twins had Apollo admitted that his own mother had died in childbirth and that that was the main reason he had been so concerned about her. Luckily the twins had been born only a couple of weeks early by a C-section and neither they nor Pixie had had any health concerns. Her brother's little boy had been born in the summer and Patrick and his little family now lived in Scotland where Apollo had found her brother a better-paying job. Patrick was still attending Gamblers Anonymous meetings regularly.

Springing upright, Apollo closed a hand over Pixie's and walked her out to the landing, leaving the twins in the care of their nannies. 'I have a present for you,' he proffered.

'Now? But tomorrow is Christmas Day!' she protested.

'Every day feels like Christmas with you, *agapi mou*,' Apollo traded. 'And Vito and Holly will be arriving in a couple of hours.'

'My goodness, is it that time already?' Pixie asked in an anxious voice. 'I should check the—'

'No,' Apollo stated firmly. 'You don't need to check anything. The house is decked out like a Christmas fair. The gifts are wrapped and our staff have mealtimes covered.'

Pixie gazed down at her gorgeous sparkling Christmas tree in the hall and she slowly smiled. He was right. Everything was done. It had become a tradition that every year the two young families shared Christmas and this year it was Apollo and Pixie who were playing host because Holly was pregnant again with her third child and she wanted to take it easy and be a guest. And although Pixie and Holly didn't compete over who could put on the best festive show, high expectations did add a certain inevitable stress to the preparations. In any case, the whole house was looking marvellous. Holly was good at design and she had put together some colour schemes for the island villa and it was a much more welcoming house now that the bland beiges had been swept away and replaced with clear bright and subtle colours.

'Bed?' Pixie whispered to her husband because the arrival of guests, even if they were best friends, did put certain restrictions on what they could and couldn't do.

'You see, this is why I want to be married to you for ever and ever,' Apollo declared as he swept her up into his arms. 'You think like I do...'

Sometimes he was naïve, Pixie thought fondly. It wasn't that she thought the same way as he did. It was more simply that she could never resist his sex appeal. He was dressed down for the day too in well-washed jeans and a sweater, but her amazing male still took her breath away with one wicked, wolfish smile. He just made her happy. In bed, out of bed, as a husband, as a father, he was all she had ever dreamt of and a couple of years of marriage had only increased his pulling power. His patient approach with Hector had taught her a lot about the man she had married. At heart he was kind and loving and good.

Hector and his little Greek shadow, another terrier called Sausage, followed them upstairs.

Apollo slid a diamond eternity ring onto Pixie's already crowded finger. Her hands sparkled with a plethora of rings and she chose which ones to wear every morning. He liked to buy her stuff and she knew it was because she was rarely out of her husband's thoughts when he was away from her. He kept his business trips brief and, if he could, took them all out on the yacht and did business on *Circe* where he could still have his family around him.

'It's beautiful,' she told him gently, grey eyes silver bright with love and understanding because she had gradually come to see that having his own family meant everything to Apollo. He had longed to have a loving family when he was a child and had been sadly disillusioned by his father's disastrous remarriages. Creating his own family as an adult had given him a kind of rebirth, allowing him to grow into the man he might have become had he had a less dysfunctional childhood.

'No, you're the jewel who outshines every setting,' Apollo insisted, claiming her soft mouth in a hungry, demanding kiss that sent little shivers quivering through her. He pinned her to the bed, gazing down at her with unashamed satisfaction. 'Do you think Vito and Holly are aiming for a football team in the kid department?' he asked curiously.

'I wouldn't be surprised,' she said with a grin. 'But it'll be a year or two before I want another one. Tobias and Sofia are exhausting.'

'Almost as demanding as their mother,' Apollo groaned, intercepting the fingers running along a lean, muscular thigh and carrying her tiny hand to a rather more responsive area. 'But I *love* that about you.'

Pixie looked up into glittering green enticement fringed by black. 'I love you, Apollo.'

'Isn't that fortunate? Because I'm keeping you for ever,' he admitted thickly.

And later when their guests had arrived and every room seemed to be awash with overexcited exploring children and equally excited dogs, the adults settled down with drinks and snacks and Pixie curled comfortably up beneath Apollo's protective arm and admired the sparkling lanterns glowing on the Christmas tree. It promised to be another wonderful Christmas and she was sincerely grateful for the happy ending she had found with the man she loved.

* * * * *

MILLS & BOON®
Hardback – December 2016

ROMANCE

A Di Sione for the Greek's Pleasure	Kate Hewitt
The Prince's Pregnant Mistress	Maisey Yates
The Greek's Christmas Bride	Lynne Graham
The Guardian's Virgin Ward	Caitlin Crews
A Royal Vow of Convenience	Sharon Kendrick
The Desert King's Secret Heir	Annie West
Married for the Sheikh's Duty	Tara Pammi
Surrendering to the Vengeful Italian	Angela Bissell
Winter Wedding for the Prince	Barbara Wallace
Christmas in the Boss's Castle	Scarlet Wilson
Her Festive Doorstep Baby	Kate Hardy
Holiday with the Mystery Italian	Ellie Darkins
White Christmas for the Single Mum	Susanne Hampton
A Royal Baby for Christmas	Scarlet Wilson
Playboy on Her Christmas List	Carol Marinelli
The Army Doc's Baby Bombshell	Sue MacKay
The Doctor's Sleigh Bell Proposal	Susan Carlisle
The Baby Proposal	Andrea Laurence
Maid Under the Mistletoe	Maureen Child

MILLS & BOON®
Large Print – December 2016

ROMANCE

The Di Sione Secret Baby	Maya Blake
Carides's Forgotten Wife	Maisey Yates
The Playboy's Ruthless Pursuit	Miranda Lee
His Mistress for a Week	Melanie Milburne
Crowned for the Prince's Heir	Sharon Kendrick
In the Sheikh's Service	Susan Stephens
Marrying Her Royal Enemy	Jennifer Hayward
An Unlikely Bride for the Billionaire	Michelle Douglas
Falling for the Secret Millionaire	Kate Hardy
The Forbidden Prince	Alison Roberts
The Best Man's Guarded Heart	Katrina Cudmore

HISTORICAL

Sheikh's Mail-Order Bride	Marguerite Kaye
Miss Marianne's Disgrace	Georgie Lee
Her Enemy at the Altar	Virginia Heath
Enslaved by the Desert Trader	Greta Gilbert
Royalist on the Run	Helen Dickson

MEDICAL

The Prince and the Midwife	Robin Gianna
His Pregnant Sleeping Beauty	Lynne Marshall
One Night, Twin Consequences	Annie O'Neil
Twin Surprise for the Single Doc	Susanne Hampton
The Doctor's Forbidden Fling	Karin Baine
The Army Doc's Secret Wife	Charlotte Hawkes

MILLS & BOON®
Hardback – January 2017

ROMANCE

A Deal for the Di Sione Ring	Jennifer Hayward
The Italian's Pregnant Virgin	Maisey Yates
A Dangerous Taste of Passion	Anne Mather
Bought to Carry His Heir	Jane Porter
Married for the Greek's Convenience	Michelle Smart
Bound by His Desert Diamond	Andie Brock
A Child Claimed by Gold	Rachael Thomas
Defying Her Billionaire Protector	Angela Bissell
Her New Year Baby Secret	Jessica Gilmore
Slow Dance with the Best Man	Sophie Pembroke
The Prince's Convenient Proposal	Barbara Hannay
The Tycoon's Reluctant Cinderella	Therese Beharrie
Falling for Her Wounded Hero	Marion Lennox
The Surgeon's Baby Surprise	Charlotte Hawkes
Santiago's Convenient Fiancée	Annie O'Neil
Alejandro's Sexy Secret	Amy Ruttan
The Doctor's Diamond Proposal	Annie Claydon
Weekend with the Best Man	Leah Martyn
One Baby, Two Secrets	Barbara Dunlop
The Tycoon's Secret Child	Maureen Child

MILLS & BOON®
Large Print – January 2017

ROMANCE

To Blackmail a Di Sione	Rachael Thomas
A Ring for Vincenzo's Heir	Jennie Lucas
Demetriou Demands His Child	Kate Hewitt
Trapped by Vialli's Vows	Chantelle Shaw
The Sheikh's Baby Scandal	Carol Marinelli
Defying the Billionaire's Command	Michelle Conder
The Secret Beneath the Veil	Dani Collins
Stepping into the Prince's World	Marion Lennox
Unveiling the Bridesmaid	Jessica Gilmore
The CEO's Surprise Family	Teresa Carpenter
The Billionaire from Her Past	Leah Ashton

HISTORICAL

Stolen Encounters with the Duchess	Julia Justiss
The Cinderella Governess	Georgie Lee
The Reluctant Viscount	Lara Temple
Taming the Tempestuous Tudor	Juliet Landon
Silk, Swords and Surrender	Jeannie Lin

MEDICAL

Taming Hollywood's Ultimate Playboy	Amalie Berlin
Winning Back His Doctor Bride	Tina Beckett
White Wedding for a Southern Belle	Susan Carlisle
Wedding Date with the Army Doc	Lynne Marshall
Capturing the Single Dad's Heart	Kate Hardy
Doctor, Mummy... Wife?	Dianne Drake

MILLS & BOON®

Why shop at millsandboon.co.uk?

Each year, thousands of romance readers find their perfect read at millsandboon.co.uk. That's because we're passionate about bringing you the very best romantic fiction. Here are some of the advantages of shopping at www.millsandboon.co.uk:

* **Get new books first**—you'll be able to buy your favourite books one month before they hit the shops

* **Get exclusive discounts**—you'll also be able to buy our specially created monthly collections, with up to 50% off the RRP

* **Find your favourite authors**—latest news, interviews and new releases for all your favourite authors and series on our website, plus ideas for what to try next

* **Join in**—once you've bought your favourite books, don't forget to register with us to rate, review and join in the discussions

Visit **www.millsandboon.co.uk**
for all this and more today!